Ndakaripa

K B Manyame

ISBN: 978-1-990239-21-2

Contents

Synopsis

"Winona Manyame's office ... Winona speaking ..."

She breathed into the phone

"Good. My name is Ndakaripa Nemapare. I understand you are a Private Investigator ... 'a good one' ... to quote my best friend's words."

The female voice on the other end paused

Winona smiled into the phone and said

"Thank you for the complement, Maam.”

Then curiosity getting the better of her could not help but ask

“May I know the name of your best friend who referred you to me, please?"

A twinkle was in her eye

"Ruramisai ... Ruramisai Nematumbai ..."

The female voice replied

"You come highly recommended. She said you helped her solve a Gutu mysterious case last year that had baffled them for months."

Winona smiled and said

"Oh, yes ... Ruramisai ... she is my College mate and friend. And yes, I did help her out with the case you are referring to."

"I would like to make an appointment with you at the earliest date possible, please. There is a case I would like you to investigate”

The female voice continued. Winona reached for her diary, flipped through it, found the page she had been looking for, read through it and said

"I have an opening next week ..."

"Can't we make it earlier than that ...?!! Could you squeeze me in, say tomorrow ...?"

The female voice cut in. Winona hesitated

"Eh ... eh ..."

"Its urgent that I meet with you. Lives are at stake ..."

The female voice insisted. Winona hesitated again

"Tomorrow ... ? ... Mmmm ... "

And she flipped through the page

"I'm afraid I am totally booked ..."

"Please ... please ... even if we make the appointment after hours ...I am willing to pay you double your normal fees ..."

The lady insisted

Winona hesitated

"Mmmm ..."

"Five times your normal fees ...?"

The lady bargained

Winona tried to say

"It's not about the money, Maam ..."

"Ten times ...!!"

The lady was not taking 'No' for an answer. From the way she was behaving, she clearly needed her case, whatever it was, to be solved quickly. Winona sensed the sense of urgency in the woman. She scanned through her diary again. She was trying to find a slot where she could squeeze the lady in

From the way she was behaving, she clearly needed her Case, whatever it was, to be solved quickly. Why was this lady so anxious to meet up with Winona?!!

What Case could she want resolved so badly and that quickly that she could not wait a few days until Winona was free?

The Second in The Winona Manyame Mysteries, P. I Winona Manyame, is hired by Ndakaripa Nemapare, a wealthy tycoon to investigate on both the mysterious disappearance of her little girl, Tanatswa; and some mysterious occurrences in her home.

The Nemapare household is plagued with strange, dark supernatural forces which haunt and traumatise Ndakaripa and Dambudzo for years. Who or what could be causing these strange occurrences ... and why ...?!! Will Winona be able to get to solve this 'cold' Case?

The investigation plunges her deep into the mysterious, secretive, dangerous, dark world of ritual sacrifices and brutal killings in Harare. Secrets, danger, mystery, deceit lurks within the hearts, homes and heads of the characters in this heart wrenching Story.

Get ready to be transported into the world of superstition, satanism, ritual sacrifices and evil deeds. Ndakaripa is a story that will baffle you, wrench at your heart, play with your emotions and leave you calling for more!!

Chapter 1 - Svuu ... ko ndianiko uyo nhai?!!

"*Hesvu*!! *Ndi* Dambudzo *here wandaona apo achinanaidzana naMai Tanatswa*?!!" [Goodness!! Is that Dambudzo I just saw there serenading with the mother of Tanatswa?]

Takesure whispered to his wife in a conspiratorial way. Then squinting his eyes to get a better view, added

"A a ... the waiter has just seated them!!"

Zorai looked around in the same conspiratorial manner towards the direction Takesure was referring to. She was trying to catch a glimpse of the above-mentioned 'culprits'. As she turned around, she caught sight of two individuals, deep in conversation on the other table. They were so engrossed in each other, they were totally oblivious of anyone around them. Much to her utter disbelief, *zvikara* [culprits] were holding hands!!

"*Hezvo ...!! Ndivo nhai !!*"
[Goodness!! It's them!!]

Zorai exclaimed in a low, but urgent voice. The couple was having lunch in their favourite restaurant in Harare. It wasn't a weekend ... no ... but during a week day ... a Wednesday. Zorai and Takesure were having their mandatory Date Night ... only it wasn't 'night', but during the day. Throughout their twenty eight year marriage, they had maintained this tradition as a way of keeping their romance alive. Boy ... and was it alive!!

It was kicking, screaming and dancing with vitality; loads to talk about, what with now the added spice of having something to gossip about!! The restaurant, *Munhira Grill*, was situated right in the Central Business District of Harare. It was always full, even during lunch hours, right in the middle of the week.

One could see waiters dressed smartly in their sunflower yellow half aprons, darting from one table to another. For that touch of added health consciousness, they wore matching chef-like hats. For ease of flight from one table to the next, they wore white soft soled shoes.

To everyone's surprise who spotted the soles for the first time, they noticed that they matched the colour of the aprons and hats!! Anyone who knew their style recognized that the shoes were a Harper Matambanadzo brand. The uniforms - white in colour - had been designed by The House of Kudandaya.

It was a famous Fashion House, not only in Zimbabwe, but in Southern Africa, Europe and The Americas. Dambudzo and Mai Tanatswa had been talk of the family for years ... until they separated and consequently divorced more than ten years before.

Zorai glanced at the couple again. True enough, the two love birds were now placing their Order. The waiter was scribbling it on his A5 Notepad and nodding vigorously. From the way the waiter was behaving, the duo must have placed a large and expensive order ... 'possibly Champagne on ice ...!!'

Zorai winked wickedly at her co-conspirator, her beloved husband. Like his wife, Takesure was gazing with hooded eyes at the duo seated on the other table.

"Do you think we should go to their table and greet them?"

Takesure whispered

Zorai reached deep into her female intuition and retrieved what she needed. As a result, she shook her head and said

"No, I think lets give them their privacy. Something tells me they are celebrating something ..."

Takesure nodded and said

"Maybe you are right, *mudiwa* [honey] ..."

Then noticing their own waiter approaching their table, the two conspirators turned and flipped through their Menu...

Chapter 2 - The Call

"Winona Manyame's office ... Winona speaking ..."

She breathed into the phone

"Good. My name is Ndakaripa Nemapare. I understand you are a Private Investigator ... 'a good one' ... to quote my best friend's words."

The female voice on the other end paused Winona smiled into the phone and said

"Thank you for the complement, Maam.”

Then curiosity getting the better of her could not help but ask

“May I know the name of your best friend who referred you to me, please?"

A twinkle was in her eye

"Ruramisai ... Ruramisai Nematumbai ..."

The female voice replied

"You come highly recommended. She said you helped her solve a Gutu mysterious case last year that had baffled them for months."

Winona smiled and said

"Oh, yes ... Ruramisai ... she is my College mate and friend. And yes, I did help her out with the case you are referring to."

"I would like to make an appointment with you at the earliest date possible, please. There is a case I would like you to investigate "

The female voice continued Winona reached for her diary, flipped through it, found the page she had been looking for, read through it and said

"I have an opening next week ..."

"Can't we make it earlier than that ...?!! Could you squeeze me in, say tomorrow ...?"

The female voice cut in. Winona hesitated

"Eh ... eh ..."

"Its urgent that I meet with you. Lives are at stake ..."

The female voice insisted Winona hesitated again

"Tomorrow ... ? ... Mmmm ... "

And she flipped through the page

"I'm afraid I am totally booked ..."

"Please ... please ... even if we make the appointment after hours ... I am willing to pay you double your normal fees ..."

The lady insisted Winona hesitated

"Mmmm ..."

"Five times your normal fees ...?"

The lady bargained Winona tried to say

"It's not about the money, Maam ..."

"Ten times ...!!"

The lady was not taking 'No' for an answer. From the way she was behaving, she clearly needed her case, whatever it was, to be solved quickly. Winona sensed the sense of urgency in the woman she scanned through her diary again. She was trying to find a slot where she could squeeze the lady in

Spotting a slot, she said

"We could meet at *Munhira Grill* during lunch time tomorrow ..."

"Yes!! Yes!! I can make it. What time is lunch for you?"

The lady was now sounding excited and alert

"From 1pm until 2pm ..."

Winona replied

"Excellent!! Excellent! I will be there!! I will arrive early and book us a table"

The lady was now sounding cheerful

"Alright"

Winona said carefully

"Perfect!! When you get to the restaurant, just ask the waiter to usher you to Ndakaripa Nemapare table."

The lady added

"Ok Till tomorrow then ..."

Winona said

"Looking forward to meeting you tomorrow. Bye"

The lady spoke and disconnected the line

Winona replaced the receiver back on its cradle. She swivelled in her chair, a reflective expression on her face.

'Talk about a woman who is used to having things her own way ...!!'

Winona chuckled to herself.

'I wonder what this is all about ...'

Winona thought as she got back to her work. She hadn't been lying when she told Ndakaripa that she was swamped. Her office had been getting busier and busier by the week.

She was actually thinking of hiring an Assistant to share the work load. She glanced at her in-tray. She already had received a bunch of Curriculum Vitaes but had not yet found the time to go through them. She shook her head. Then another thought hit her ...

'Ruramisai ... her good friend ...'

She smiled

'So sweet of her to link her up like this!!'

She must remember to call her one of these days!! Gutu sounded so far away from Harare!!, she thought

----

"Madam please wait your turn. We have a full house this afternoon."

The friendly waiter at *Munhira Grill* tried to restrain her from going further inside the restaurant

"Actually, I think the lady I am supposed to meet is already here ... "

Winona hesitated

"Her name is Mrs Ndakaripa Nemapare ... ?"

She smiled back looking around the restaurant curiously, wondering which of the ladies dining alone could be the lady in-question.

"Oh, yes!! You mean the owner of this restaurant?!!"

The waiter smiled even more broadly. Winona looked surprised

'Owner of THIS restaurant ?!!'

"Come this way ... She is already waiting for you on another table ..."

The waiter was already leading the way. Winona followed. As usual, *Munhira Grill* was full to capacity. Diners were enjoying their lunch with soft lunchtime music drifting through some powerful speakers embedded in the ceiling and floors, creating an ethereal surround sound effect.

'What was their secret?'

Winona wondered

She had dodged a long queue snaking all the way from outside the Mall all the way into the restaurant. What surprised and baffled Winona was that there were many restaurants around this Mall, yet people preferred to wait in line for 10 to 20 minutes just to be given a Table.

Other restaurants stood empty whilst *Munhira Grill* could hardly cope with the volume of traffic of customers that preferred to dine in their restaurant!! It was remarkable!!

After all, it wasn't like their prices were lower than the other restaurants. In fact, they were on the pricey side!! Winona suspected the secret to *Munhira Grill*'s success lay in their Chef.

'Soothing ... classy ... ethereal ...'

Winona thought as she followed the waiter Thank goodness she had worn her heels!! A real confidence booster!!

She heaved a sigh of relief. After navigating and weaving through a number of tables, Winona found herself on the quieter side of the restaurant. It was more private, overlooking a stunning piazza. Winona had been to this restaurant a number of times, but she had never been to THIS PART of the restaurant!!

If she had thought what she had just seen as she weaved her way through the restaurant a few seconds ago was ... 'stunning ... classy ... ethereal ...'; to this section of the restaurant multiply that by three!!

"Wow!!"

Winona could not help herself. The waiter smiled and said softly in that manner and ambiance that befits a restaurant atmosphere as this

"Everyone who sees this part of the restaurant for the first time, says the exact same thing!!"

He looked proud of his surroundings.The waiter directed her towards a table nearest the glass facade view. A lady was seated there, but when she saw the waiter and Winona approach her table, she stood up, smiled and walked quickly towards them. Her arms were outstretched in the form of a greeting. Without waiting to be formally introduced, she hastened to say

"I take it you are Winona Manyame of Manyame and Manyame Private Investigators ...?"

"Yes, Maam. And I take it you are Mrs Nemapare ...?"

Winona accepted the handshake

"Please, let's drop the formalities ... Call me Ndakaripa. That's my given name. Mrs Nemapare is my mother-in-law!!"

She winked wickedly Winona could not help but be intrigued and taken by this woman. Her openness, friendliness and cheerfulness was not something you saw everyday ... well at least not in Winona's day, anyway. Most of the clients she came across were so preoccupied and overwhelmed with their problems they could hardly display a smile, let alone come across as cheerful!!

"Ok, Ndakaripa!!"

Winona smiled

"You can call me Winona ..."

The two ladies smiled at each other. An instant camaraderie was developed. The waiter watched all this exchange patiently, with a half smile pasted to the two corners of his lips. As the two ladies walked to the table Ndakaripa had already reserved, the waiter followed and helped, first, his boss into the seat; then Winona.

Not one to miss anything, Winona observed this with silent interest. Clearly Ndakaripa was liked by her employees ... well ... this one ... to be exact!!, Winona thought

"William, can you give us a minute to get acquainted ... unless of course you want to Order something to drink ...?"

Ndakaripa smiled at Winona. Winona said

"I'll have a Mukai on the rocks, please"

"Good choice!!"

Ndakaripa smiled

"And I'll have my usual, please, William ..."

"Very good, Maam ..."

William bowed slightly and walked away Winona looked at the companion facing her ... a potential client and blurted

"When I mentioned *Munhira Grill* yesterday on the phone, you did not tell me that you own this place ...!!"

Ndakaripa laughed ... a light, soft, beautiful sound.

"William ...!!"

She blurted

"I know its him who told you!!"

And she giggled

"Yes, I own this place ... my husband and I ..."

Ndakaripa seemed to sober up at the mention of her husband.

"I didn't tell you because I thought I would explain my life story to you when we met ..."

Winona nodded She was looking at Ndakaripa curiously. When Winona looked at her ... up, close and personal ... Winona noticed fine lines under Ndakaripa's eyes ... She had not noticed them a few minutes before as they met and introduced themselves to each other. She was a forty something woman ... had a sophisticated, refined and polished look about her. She clearly exuded wealth ...

'No wonder she is willing to pay me as much as ten times my usual fee ...!!'

Winona blinked. Money was not an object as far as this lady was concerned.

'I wonder what the problem is ...?'

Winona thought to herself

'Wondering husband, perhaps ...?'

She mused to herself. In her line of work, she had discovered, much to her chagrin, that women in such high places with money to burn usually had problems of this nature. The woman facing her was also studying her ...

'Beautiful ... no ... beautiful was a far cry to describe the woman sitting next to her ... a goddess ... was more like it. The woman had the most beautiful face she had ever seen ... everything proportional ... the jawline ... the eyes ... the mouth ... even the ears in proportion to the head. And she was tall too ...

When they had first met, Ndakaripa had noticed, much to her surprise, how tall Winona was ... 6 foot something ... And in those elegant heels ... she was a real stunner!!

"Have you ever thought of becoming a Model on the Runway, Winona?"

Ndakaripa surprised Winona with her question

"I own a Fashion House. We showcase our *haute couture* in Milan, Paris, Harare, Durban."

Winona laughed and said

"Goodness, no!! I have never thought of it!!"

Then giggled wickedly and said

"I don't think I am pretty enough!! The height? ... maybe ... but the facial features ... ehhhh ... NO!!"

And she giggled again, much to the delight of her companion

"'Not pretty enough' ? !! Are you kidding me?!!! You are a real knock out!!"

Ndakaripa produced that ethereal, mirth like laugh again But Winona was not buying it

"You flatter me!!"

And laughed

"I am a Fashion Designer and own a Fashion Magazine ... I should know!!"

Ndakaripa gave Winona a serious look.

"Kkk ..."

Winona laughed Just then, William brought their drinks.

"A Mukai on the rocks, for you!!"

He said as he placed the crystal glass next to Winona

"And a Panashe on the rocks for you!!"

He said as he placed the crystal glass next to Ndakaripa

"Thank you"

The two women said simultaneously William smiled and said

"Are you ready to place your Order now, or should I come back after a few minutes?"

Ndakaripa glanced at Winona and on impulse said

"You just must try Chef Eric's lunch special today!! It's a to die for treat ...!! And don't worry, lunch is on the house. It's the least I can do after you have been so magnanimous and agreed to see me on such short notice. I know you are swamped!"

"Chef's special? ..."

Winona smiled

"I always want to try such special cuisine ..."

Then with a fling of her hand said

"Bring it on ...!! Let's see ..."

She was feeling excited already. This lunch date was turning out to be much more adventurous than she had initially anticipated. She had been dreading it but now, she was enjoying it ... Chef Eric was famous ... well known and regarded all over the country and region as one of the best Chefs. His dishes were unique, full of flavour and healthy too!! Diners travelled long distances just to come and taste his specialty dishes.

Winona's taste buds were watering already ...

Chapter 3 - The Chat

"You would not believe who I saw during lunch today ..."

Zorai was speaking in her mobile. She was now back at the office. Takesure had gone to fetch the kids from school. He was having a Business Meeting with a Client afterwards. Zorai was the Human Resources Manager at one of the big supermarkets at Sam Levy Village in Borrowdale, Harare. Lunch with hubbie had been a blast, especially now that she was armed to the teeth with 'news' ... CORRECTION ... 'information'!!

"Who did you see?"

A female voice on the other end of the line asked. The lady sounded equally excited; her 'information' tentacles having been activated by the tone in Zorai's voice.

"Come to my office, if you want to know more ...!!"

Zorai continued in that conspiratorial voice

"Am on it!! Give me five minutes ...!!"

The female voice said and disconnected the line. Zorai smiled as she put her mobile phone down on her desk. Her heart was beating fast. She had exciting 'information' to share.

Whereas other people got excited when they sealed that business deal or obtained that latest acquisition in a Merger, Zorai got the same excitement when she had 'information' to share. The adrenaline rush was the same. And this 'information' could not wait!! She had to confide in her bossom buddy - Upenyu

Upenyu worked as a Cashier downstairs in the supermarket. The two had been buddies for more than half their lives. They had met on their way from school one afternoon. From the uniforms they were wearing, they had realized that they learnt at the same school and were in the same Grade, only different class.

Whereas Zorai was in Ms Chade's Class; Upenyu was in Ms Dube's Class. They both loved Music, that explained why they were now walking home three hours after all the other pupils had left.

Upenyu had been in the process of being bullied by a boy of their same age by the name of Mabasa. Zorai had come to her rescue by beating the boy in question to a pulp. They had been inseparable ever since. Zorai and Upenyu did everything together.

Whether it was attending Music Classes... the two were always together... Whether it was playing Tennis... the two would be in the Tennis Court together ... Whether it was attending Prize Giving Day Ceremony ... the two would sit side by side ...

Always conniving ... always gossiping ... always giggling ...

'Attached to the hip those two ...!!', their mothers used to quib

'More like twins ...!!', their husbands would laugh Surely enough, five minutes later, Upenyu was breathless, knocking on Zorai's door. She had chosen the stairs instead of the lift. A good exercise never hurt anybody, she had thought. Anyway she spent way too much time seated on that Cashier's Swivel Chair!!, Upenyu reasoned with herself

"Come in ..."

A voice said Upenyu opened the door and walked in Zorai looked up and smiled

"Taking the stairs again, I see ...!!"

She quibbed Upenyu just nodded

She could not speak She needed to catch her breath. Climbing 46 flight of stairs was not a joke, especially in heels!!

"Do sit down ..."

Zorai offered Upenyu thankfully obliged She sank heavily into one of the two seats facing Zorai over her desk. Zorai poured her a glass of water and handed it over to her It was ice cold. That's how she liked it. Upenyu thankfully downed the ice cold water, munching the ice in the process. Zorai grimaced

"I don't know how you do it ... Munching ice ...!!"

Upenyu grinned She felt better. Ice was one of her addictions ... She didn't know what she would do without it.

"Aahhh ... !!"

She sighed happily, audibly and with relish, more for eliciting a response from her friend, than anything else. Zorai grimaced, but a wicked expression was on her face. Afterall, her most favourite person was here ...

"On the mobile, you said you had something to tell me ...?"

Upenyu looked Zorai full in the face

"Spill ...!! I only have ten minutes ...I asked Bill to cover for me ..."

"Ok ..."

Zorai sat herself more comfortably in her chair She looked at her friend and said

"Whilst Takesure and I were having lunch this afternoon ... you know our Weekly Lunch Date ..."

"Yes ..."

Upenyu nodded She was aware of her friend and hubby's weekly Lunch Date.

"You would not guess who we saw having lunch together at our usual restaurant ...?"

Zorai paused for full effect

"Tell me ... "

Upenyu was impatient

"Guess ..."

Zorai's eyes twinkled

She was playing for time She wanted Upenyu to marinate in her own curiosity

"Oh, you know I am not good at this guessing game!!"

Upenyu raised her shoulders in frustration. The marinating was working!! Zorai's eyes sparkled even more with mischief. She was enjoying every minute. She waited a bit more. Upenyu fidgeted in her seat. She glared at her friend. Zorai could be so infuriating sometimes!! Satisfied that her friend had stewed long enough in curiosity, Zorai finally cut to the chase

"Mmmm ... Dambudzo and Ndakaripa Nemapare ..."

"What?!"

Upenyu exclaimed. She had expected some juicy news but not THIS juicy!!

"Are you sure?!!"

Upenyu managed

"As sure as I am seated here ..."

Zorai said

"When you say 'having lunch together' ... you mean eating together together or having lunch in the same restaurant?!! ..."

Upenyu had an incredible look on her face

"I mean eating together together ..."

Zorai confirmed

"But ... but I thought those two split up more than a decade ago?!!"

Upenyu exclaimed

"That's what we thought too ...!!"

Zorai shook her head. There was silence in the room.

"Ei ...!!"

Upenyu finally exclaimed Zorai shook her head again Clearly both women were deep in thought.

"Miracles never cease to happen ...!!"

Upenyu exclaimed

"Do you think the two are back together ...?!! Is it possible that Ndakaripa was able to forgive Dambudzo after all that drama that occurred more than ten years ago ...?!!"

Upenyu looked aghast

"I absolutely have no idea, but from the looks of it, the two looked friendly enough ..."

Zorai shrugged

"Miracles never cease ...!!"

Upenyu repeated

"Miracles never cease indeed ...!!"

Zorai looked at her friend They both shook their heads ...

Chapter 4 - The Meet Up

"The reason I asked you to meet me this afternoon is because I need your help with something ..."

Ndakaripa began Winona put her fork down, wiped her mouth with a white napkin, looked at Ndakaripa and said

"I am all ears ..."

"My husband, Dambudzo, and I own many businesses. Besides this restaurant, we also own a Fashion House, a Fashion Magazine; a fleet of Kombis that ply the Harare - Plumtree route as well as the Harare - Mutare route. We also own a franchise comprising Petrol Stations and Supermarkets."

Ndakaripa hesitated

"Go on. I am listening."

Winona encouraged

"All this sounds glamorous when viewed from outside, but from the inside, it's another story"

Ndakaripa continued

"Go on ..."

Winona kept on looking at the other woman

"You see, Dambudzo and I got married straight from College. We were young then, both in our early twenties. We were penniless, broke and did not like our jobs. I worked as a Secretary at a Construction Firm here in Harare. It paid peanuts. Dambudzo worked as a Petrol Attendant at one of the Fuel Stations in Harare. His pay was even more menial than mine. The first five years of our marriage was fraught with financial troubles of one form or another. Dambudzo and I would bicker about money nonstop.

Three years into our marriage, I conceived. Nine months later, I gave birth to a beautiful bouncy baby girl. We named her Tanatswa. She was such a healthy, happy baby ... She brought joy and excitement into our family. Two years later, I conceived again and gave birth, this time to a beautiful bouncy baby boy. We named him Tanaka. "

Ndakaripa paused. She was looking sad, all of a sudden Winona was surprised to see tears pool in Ndakaripa's eyes. She instinctively reached for her hand to comfort her. Ndakaripa seemed to have retreated somewhere far. Winona watched the play of emotions on Ndakaripa's face.

She wondered what had suddenly caused the change in her mood. In her line of work, she had learnt that it was best to allow the Client to take their time when letting out and revealing what it is that was irking them. So she patiently waited. Ndakaripa was looking at her plate. Food seemed to be the furthest thing on her mind right now.

After a few minutes, she seemed to come back. She actually had to rouse herself to the present. She blinked and seeing Winona watching her with concern, smiled sadly and said

"You see our eldest child disappeared when she was five. Dambudzo was supposed to pick her up from Nursery that day, but he said he forgot. By the time I got home that evening, it was already late. Tanatswa was not yet home.

I assumed she was with her father. But when Dambudzo arrived two hours later, he arrived alone. I asked him where our daughter was; that is when he panicked and exclaimed that he had totally forgotten to pick her up!"

Ndakaripa sniffed Winona frowned and said

"What time was he supposed to fetch her from Nursery?"

"One o'clock, during his Lunch Break"

Ndakaripa replied

"Ok. What time did you get back from work?"

Winona asked

"Eight in the evening "

Ndakaripa replied

"And what time did your husband get back?"

Winona frowned. Something did not feel right

"Ten"

Ndakaripa replied

"So that means you discovered that Tanatswa had not been picked up by her father, nine hours later!!"

Winona blinked

"Yes"

Ndakaripa blinked back

"I am curious ... how come her Nursery did not call either you or her father when they realized that she had not been picked up?"

Winona frowned again

"You see, that's just it ... The Nursery said a man claiming to be Dambudzo's cousin picked her up."

Ndakaripa's voice quivered with emotion

"What?!! But that's highly unusual, isn't it?!!"

Winona could not help but exclaim

"Don't Nurseries have strict instructions not to release kids to anyone except the designated Parent or Guardian?!!"

"Yes, you are right, they do. But the Nursery said they had seen Dambudzo with this supposed cousin once or twice whilst picking Tanatswa up; so when this time he came alone, they did not hesitate to hand her over to him."

Ndakaripa revealed

"And had he? ... Asked this cousin to pick up Tanatswa?"

Winona looked directly at Ndakaripa

"Dambudzo said he did not know what the Nursery was talking about. As far as he was concerned, he never brought anyone when he was picking up our little girl"

Ndakaripa looked at Winona Winona remained silent for a minute, trying to digest and ruminate on all she had just heard; then asked

"What was the name of this supposed cousin?"

"The Nursery could not provide us with a name "

Ndakaripa looked forlorn

"All of this is very strange to me"

Winona shook her head Ndakaripa continued

"It was very strange for me too when I first heard about it."

"Was there ever an investigation to look into her disappearance?"

Winona asked

"Yes. When we discovered that our daughter was missing, we immediately called the Police and reported it. They carried out their full investigations but came up with zero leads."

Ndakaripa was now sobbing

"But surely, a child cannot just varnish without a trace!! Someone, somewhere must have seen her!!"

Winona exclaimed, more to herself than to Ndakaripa. Ndakaripa remained silent

"You said Tanatswa disappeared when she was five? How long have you two been married?"

Winona asked

"Eighteen years."

Ndakaripa replied

"That means Tanatswa disappeared ten years ago?"

Winona enquired

"Yes"

Ndakaripa said

"That was a long time ago. Why are you coming to me now after such a long time and what do you want me to assist you with?"

Winona asked

"Yes, it was a long time ago. The reason I am coming to you now is that in the last nine years, I have been experiencing strange paranormal activities."

Ndakaripa stopped She shook her head as if to try and clear it.

"Strange paranormal activities ... like ...?"

Winona sat up in her chair This was becoming intriguing.

"Late at night when we are asleep, I am awakened by voices ..."

Ndakaripa hesitated

"Voices ...?!"

Winona repeated

"Yes ... voices ... and footsteps ..."

Ndakaripa treaded carefully

"Goodness!!"

Winona felt goose bumps creep throughout her skin

"Yes ... The voices sound like that of a little girl ... giggling ...Usually I am awoken by this giggling. When I get up to investigate, I hear footsteps running along the corridor ... The tap tap sound sounds like that of a little girl wearing shoes ..."

Ndakaripa frowned

"Have you actually seen this little girl?"

Winona asked

"That's just it ... I haven't!! I just hear it."

Ndakaripa said

"Have you informed your husband about these strange occurrences?"

Winona asked

"Yes, a dozen times."

Ndakaripa said

"And what is his take on all this?"

Winona was curious

"He says I am imagining it and insists I go back to sleep."

Ndakaripa sighed

"Ummmm ... "

Winona beat her bottom lip

"There is more ..."

Ndakaripa cautioned

"Ok ..."

Winona raised an eyebrow

"Isn't it I told you earlier that when we first got married we were dead poor?"

Ndakaripa reminded

"Yes."

Winona nodded

"About a few months after the disappearance of Tanatswa, Dambudzo came home one day wielding a Contract in his hands."

"Contract?"

Winona frowned

"Yes. He said he had won The Tender to run a franchise ... a Petrol Station franchise. I was surprised at this for we did not have a penny to our name to give as deposit to run such a franchise.

I voiced this concern to Dambudzo and he dismissed it with a shrug of his shoulders and a 'don't worry about it. It's all taken care of.'"

Ndakaripa revealed

"Mmmm ..."

Winona looked at Ndakaripa

"From then on, all the businesses we entered into took off at a meteoric rate. I had always been passionate about Fashion. Dambudzo encouraged me to open a Fashion House. I did. Six months down the line, my label was being showcased in all the Department Stores across the country. Before we knew it, I was getting Orders from Paris, Milan, Berlin, The Middle East.

It was crazy!! I branched into a Fashion Magazine to showcase our designs in print. That too, took off. Things were moving fast. It was like everything we touched was turning to gold!! Incredible!!"

Ndakaripa shook her head in mesmerisation.

"We got into the restaurant business ... then the transport industry with Kombis plying most routes around the country. "

Ndakaripa paused. Winona sensed there was more. She remained silent

"The reason for our business success was a mystery to me as it was to my husband. Things went well for about three years, then strange and bizarre things started to happen."

"'Strange and bizarre things' ...?!!"

Winona shifted in her seat.

"Yes. We were trying for a baby, but I noticed that every time Dambudzo and I slept together, he would go into a Coma for a week."

Ndakaripa stopped

"What?!!"

Winona blurted out

"What do you mean? Coma ... how ... why ...?!!"

Winona could hardly believe her ears. Ndakaripa looked directly at Winona and said

"The Doctors could not explain it. And his vitals seemed normal, yet he would be in a Coma. It was bizarre. We didn't know what else to do; after all I didn't want to kill my husband. So we decided to abstain."

"Goodness!!"

Winona exclaimed. This Case was getting more and more bizarre by the second!! No wonder Ndakaripa had sounded urgent on the phone!!

"We haven't been together, if you know what I mean, since"

Ndakaripa confided Winona remained silent. This sure was a bizarre story.

Ndokusaka vakuru vachiti, 'chakafukidza'!!
[There is a saying, 'Strange things that happen in the dark!!]
"So what do you want me to help you with?"

Winona finally asked

"I need you to investigate on what happened to our daughter ... I know its been a long time but the strange occurrences in my home have intensified lately and I want you to look into them."

Ndakaripa said

"You think the strange voices and footsteps may be linked to your daughter's disappearance?"

Winona asked Ndakaripa did not speak. She just nodded Winona looked at the other woman who suddenly looked so vulnerable sitting there. Her heart went out to her and she said

"Consider me hired!"

Ndakaripa smiled, jumped in her chair and said

"Great!! And Thank you very much!!"

Winona smiled

"So when will you start ...?!!"

Ndakaripa beamed

Chapter 5 - To what do I owe the pleasure?

"To what do I owe the pleasure?!!"

Chief Inspector Rapingwa smiled at the beautiful lady sitting facing him in his office.

"Can't a girl just visit her friend without any ulterior motive?!!"

Winona laughed

"Naaa ... I know you too well, Winona!! You are far too busy to just pay courtesy calls ...!!"

Chief Inspector Rapingwa laughed as well. Winona rubbed her chin in a conspiratorial way

"Ok, you got me!!"

And laughed

"The reason I am here is because I need your help with a Case that happened about ten years ago ..."

Winona began

"Ten years...?...that's a rather long time ago ... I'll have to dig into my files .."

Chief Inspector Rapingwa mused

"Its a Case of the mysterious disappearance of a little girl ... five year old by the name of Tanatswa Nemapare ... She disappeared from the Nursery School she was attending at the time after her father forgot to pitch to pick her up and a 'cousin' is said to have picked her up instead ..."

Winona filled him in Chief Inspector Rapingwa frowned slightly as his little grey cells did a double take of Cases he had handled ten years before.

"I seem to remember that Case ... Tragic ... Mother was so affected by her little girl's disappearance she went into a serious depression ... had to be institutionalized for a few months ...

If my memory serves me right, the scandal hit the Headlines and The Nursery had to be shut down after the other parents went on a nationwide uproar. The State filed a Civil Lawsuit against The Nursery for negligence. The fact that they never could provide the name or contact details of the supposed 'cousin' is what got them into deep waters. The Head was found guilty and sentenced to Three Years imprisonment.

"Winona produced a low whistle and said

"Eish ... sounds like it was a big Case ... very public ...Mmmm ... I wonder why I don't remember it? ..."

"If I remember correctly, it was that time when you took a six months Leave from your work and spent it languishing at the beach in The Caribbean ..."

Chief Inspector Rapingwa filled in

"Oh ...!! THAT time?!!! ..."

Winona recalled

"Yes. From our end, when the parents filed a Missing Persons Report, we did our own investigation but came up with no leads whatsoever. It was a very strange Case bearing in mind that no one seemed to know what had happened to the child. She had simply varnished into thin air !!"

Chief Inspector Rapingwa shook his head

"You said The Nursery was shut down and The Head was imprisoned ...? ..."

Winona asked

"Yes ..."

Chief Inspector Rapingwa said

"What was the name of The Nursery School? ..."

Winona asked

"St Gabriel ..."

Chief Inspector Rapingwa replied

"And name of Head ...?"

Winona asked

"Mrs. Emilda Shoorai ..."

Chief Inspector Rapingwa replied Winona wrote this information in her A4 Leather bound Sunflower Yellow Notebook

"That's a Harper Matambanadzo brand, right?!"

Chief Inspector Rapingwa asked excitedly, pointing towards Winona's notebook.

"Yes ... why?!!"

Winona looked puzzled

"My wife, Stella, has been pressing me to buy her one for her birthday!! Problem is I have no idea where to find Harper Matambanadzo brands!! I know they are exclusive ..."

Chief Inspector Rapingwa laughed Winona laughed out loud

"Yes, the brand IS exclusive, but I can give you a contact number. You can call them and tell them you have been referred by me. You can place your Order and they can place you on their Waiting List"

Winona paused, then noticing a glint of excitement in The Chief Inspector's eyes, hastened to caution

"You'll have to be patient though, for they have a long list already of Orders and yours can take anywhere between three to six months to be delivered. That's how exclusive The Harper Matambanadzo brand is!!"

Chief Inspector Rapingwa grinned broadly

"That would be so helpful of you, Winona!! I tell you Stella would love me for life and forgive ALL my sins ... those I have already committed and those I am still to commit, if I get her this brand!!"

Winona burst out laughing. The matter at hand was momentarily forgotten as the two friends exchanged Harper Matambanadzo contact details. Chief Inspector Rapingwa danced in his chair. Winona chuckled good naturedly.

"Can I speak to Mrs Emilda Shoorai, please? ..."

Winona spoke over the phone She was back in her office

"How did you get this number?!!"

A male voice said roughly

"My name is Winona Manyame. I am the owner of Manyame and Manyame Private Investigators. I have been contracted to investigate on the disappearance of one little girl by the name of Tanatswa Nemapare ten years ago. I understand Mrs Shoorai was The Head of St Gabriel Nursery School at the time ..."

Winona trailed

"Listen lady ...!!"

The voice sounded impatient

"My wife has done her time on this Case ... she has suffered greatly ...Infact, the whole family has ... All we want now is peace and quiet ... ok?!!"

The man was almost shouting at this point. Then added

"Please ... LEAVE US ALONE!!! ..."

And disconnected the line Winona was left gaping and listening to the buzz of the disconnected line. Clearly the family had suffered enough, Winona empathised as she placed the receiver back on its cradle. Well, that was a dud ...!!, Winona shrugged Now what?!! She bit her lip

She stood up from her desk and started pacing around her office.

'Who is this 'cousin'?', Winona mused

Then a voice said

'Who was the Teacher responsible for releasing the kids that fateful day?!! That's the person I should be speaking to!!'

Winona stopped midstep. Winona reached for her telephone and dialled

"Chief Inspector Rapingwa, please ...?"

"One moment please, while I connect you ..."

A female voice said Winona said

"Thank you ..."

And heard a click, followed by a

"Chief Inspector Rapingwa speaking ..."

"Chief Inspector ... Winona here ..."

"Ah ... Hallo my good friend ..."

Chief Inspector Rapingwa smiled into the phone

"I need another favour ..."

Winona began

"Oh ...?"

Chief Inspector Rapingwa prompted

"What was the name of the teacher on duty that fateful afternoon when Tanatswa Nemapare disappeared? ... you know the teacher responsible for releasing the kids after school ...?"

Winona breathed Chief Inspector Rapingwa frowned

"Goodness, for the life of me I cannot remember. I will have to dig into our archives ... Give me a day or two ... I will get back to you ..."

"Alright ..."

Winona said. The pair disconnected the line. Winona paced again Ok, so she will know the name in a day or two. Fine. Winona tapped her pen on her left thumb.

She swivelled in her chair. She was thinking. Then a thought hit her. She suddenly had the urge to see the scene of the crime. Maybe it would give her clues as to what might have transpired on that fateful afternoon. Ten years had passed but in her years of experience as a P.I she knew that the aura always lingered at the scene the crime was committed.

She grabbed her handbag and car keys and left her office, locking it behind her in the process. She still remembered vividly where the Nursery had been located. She had passed by it a few times whilst it was still operating. It had been popular too.

Most parents would have gladly burst their bank account if it meant their child could be admitted to this erstwhile school. The school was famous for boasting the latest and most competent teachers that made use of the fanciest and futuristic learning child development techniques. Winona got into her SUV and drove.

It was one of the latest posh cars on the market. She was proud of it. It was a joy to drive. Before long, Winona was now on the highway. She was headed in the direction of Rusape. How she loved to drive along this route!!

The drive was so smooth, so effortless, so easy. She let out a joyful sigh. She looked around. Harare. How she loved this city ... the capital city of Zimbabwe. There was something about it ... the ambience ... the feel of it ...

Chapter 6 – Ndaneta

'Ahhhhh ... *ndaneta* ...!!'
[I am tired] ...!!

A voice said. Passengers ignored the sound and continued doing whatever it was they had been doing. Some were looking out through the window, enjoying the scenery. After all, the Kwekwe to Gweru Road is scenic.

Lush vegetation, loads of green grass, fresh cool air. Some were eating *chibage* [boiled white corn, slightly sautéed], whilst others were dozing. The ride was soothing that way.

"Ndaneta ...!!"

The voice said again. This time passengers looked at each other, the same question on their minds. No one spoke. The ones who had been enjoying the scenery were now looking around the van, trying to see if someone was speaking in their sleep.

The ones eating *chibage* continued feasting, although they were looking around as well in a quizzical manner. The ones dozing were now wide awake. The driver shifted uneasily in his seat. He could tell the passengers were becoming uneasy.

This was the boss' fault!! He had informed him already that whenever they had driven about 200 kilometres in this van, THIS happened!! The boss had dismissed it as the driver's over-active imagination!!

"Ndaneta ...!!"

The voice said a third time. This time one of the women passengers blurted

"Who said that?!!"

All the passengers looked at each other. They were trying to identify who had spoken. No one was sleeping anymore, so there was no chance of anyone having spoken in their sleep.

The *Windie* [The van Conductor] glared at the driver, saw the worried look in his eyes. The two exchanged conspiratorial looks. The *Windie* drawled

"Nothing to worry about, folks!! Just the engine creaking. It does that sometimes. Settle down. Let us enjoy the journey!!"

Passengers seemed to be placated by these words of assurance. They settled down. Those who had been enjoying the scenery went back to doing that. The ones who had been feasting on their *chibage* continued with their feasting.

Those who had been dozing, settled themselves more comfortably in their seats and tried to catch up on their beauty sleep before it had been rudely interrupted.

The van ploughed on. One kilometre ... two ... three ... twenty kilometres ...

They stopped for gas in Gweru. Everyone went for recess and stretch their legs. Some bought *nzungu* [roasted peanuts, slightly sautéed] to munch and snack on their journey. The journey resumed. But the voice would not relent. Twenty kilometres out of Gweru heading for Bulawayo the voice came again

"Ndaneta ...!!"

This time there was a jolt in the van. Even the Driver and *Windie* looked visibly shaken. The two men started to perspire. There was no question. The voice had come from somewhere under the engine.

"Who said that ...?!!!"

A male passenger looked around, darting his head back and forth Everyone prinned their ears to listen The driver looked back at his passengers in concern, but said nothing

This time even the *Windie* remained silent. His heart was beating a tard faster. His mouth felt dry The driver drove on for another 3 kilometres. There was total silence.

'Ahhhh ... *ndaneta* ... !!!'

The voice said again

"*Ndiani adaro* ... ?!!"
[Who said that ...?!!]

A female passenger looked around, now in a half panic

"I didn't hear anything ...!!"

The driver said cautiously

'*Ndati ndaneta* ...!!'
[I said I am tired]

The voice persisted

"I heard it ...!!"

Another male passenger looked back. A look of terror was plastered all over his face. He was seated in front on the passenger side next to the driver.

"I think you are imagining things ..."

The driver tried to placate them. It was obvious. Something was definitely amiss here. It was clear that all the driver was trying to do was hide his head in the sand 'ostrich-like' and pretend that everything was OK, when it wasn't.

He pressed his foot down on the gas pedal and the van increased speed. Everyone jerked forward as the van gathered speed and sped across the highway.

'Ndaneta ... ndaneta ... ndaneta ...!!!'

The voice persisted and let out a tired sigh. The twelve passengers looked at each other, heads darting this way and that, trying to figure out WHO had just uttered those words. But they could not identify WHO had just spoken.

Clearly the voice they had just heard was real but the physical identity of the person who had just spoken was not immediately visible to the naked eye!! What was going on here?!!, the passengers wondered

A look of panic was now on all their faces. Even those ones who had been dozing, sinking in and out of sleep became wide awake. The long drive from Harare to Bulawayo had suddenly become eventful halfway between Gweru and Bulawayo.

They had just passed the 20 kilometre peg out of Gweru heading past Antelope Park - one of the best privately owned animal sanctuaries with a lot of various animals from lions, elephants, kudus, antelopes and activities to do.

'Ndaneta ...', the voice said again

This time, it was said more in a whisper than a loud voice.

"STOP THE VAN ...!!"

One of the passengers seated at the back shouted The driver pretended not to have heard and continued pressing his foot on the gas pedal.

"I said, 'STOP THE VAN!!'", the passenger was now screaming at the top of his voice.

"I agree!! Stop the van!!"

Another female passenger agreed with her male compatriot There was a scuffle in the van as the passengers ordered the driver to stop. The driver had no choice but to lift his foot from the gas pedal and slow down.

He looked in his rear view mirror to make sure the road was clear before he indicated, slowed down until he had come to a stop at the shoulder of the road. The passenger nearest the door, reached for it. The voice said

'*Maita* ... [Thank you] ...' and sighed in relief

The passenger flung the door wide open and without thinking twice, jumped out. He ran for dear life.

The other passengers followed suite. Twelve people could be seen scattering this way and that, running away from the van as if it had caught fire and would blow up at any moment. Thank goodness there was no on-coming traffic, otherwise some of the passengers ran the high risk of being run over!!

The twelve passengers ran into the nearby bushes and hid. Only the driver and *Windie* were left standing by their van looking this way and that at the fleeing beings. They felt helpless.

"So now, what do we do?!!"

The driver rubbed his head in confusion

"Call the boss ..."

The *Windie* suggested

"Good idea ..."

The Driver agreed reaching out for his mobile. He scrawled down his Contacts, found the Contact he wanted and dialled

"Mr Nemapare ... we have a slight problem here ..."

"BREAKING NEWS ..."

A female voice on H=m2 Television News Channel reported

"Earlier today, twelve passengers travelling from Harare to Bulawayo found themselves cutting their trip short when they discovered that the van they had been travelling in was actually being driven by a *sitokoloshi*.

Sitokoloshi are dwarf-like water sprite. They are considered a mischievous and evil spirit that can become invisible by drinking water or swallowing a stone. Tokoloshes are called upon by malevolent people to cause trouble for others."

The reporter then turned away from the camera to face the passengers, who had now huddled into a group, a few feet from the still parked van.

"So, tell us ... what happened here?"

The female Reporter prompted one of the passengers

"Earlier this afternoon, I hitched a ride with *Nemapare Passenger Services*."

At this, Winona who had been listening and watching this piece of news with detached interest sat up in her seat. She was watching local news in the comfort of her lounge.

'Nemapare Passenger Services ...?!!'

She sat up She reached for her remote and increased the volume.

"... at Mbare Bus Station in Harare. We were bound for Bulawayo. Halfway through our journey, we started to hear a voice ..."

The passenger hesitated

"... a voice ...?"

The reporter repeated

"Yes ..."

Another passenger budged in The reporter trained the mike at the new entrant

"... it said '*Ndaneta* ...!!'"

The other passenger filled in

"Goodness!! Why do you think it was a *sitokoloshi* ... maybe it was one of the passengers speaking from his or her sleep ...?!!"

The reporter suggested

"No, it wasn't any of us!! There was ANOTHER person or rather 'presence' with us in that van ..."

The passenger clarified

"... and that presence was supernatural, I am sure of it ...!!"

Yet another passenger butted in. There was a kind of uproar around the passengers as each one of them spoke all at once. The reporter trained the mike at herself and said

"There you heard it from the horse's mouth. My News Crew and I visited Mbare Bus Station after this interview and gathered that other passengers are now boycotting this Passenger Service. They believe the owner is using voodoo and some other strange magic portions to get ahead in business."

Nancy Shumbayaonda reporting LIVE from Gweru ... h=m2 Television News Channel

Winona muted the television. What had she just heard?!! *Nemapare Passenger Services* was Ndakaripa and Dambudzo's business venture ... one of them. What was this she had just heard?!! She placed the remote on the crystal table, stood up and started pacing.

'*Sitokoloshi* ...?!!'

Was Ndakaripa and Dambudzo into some satanic cult ...?!! As far as Winona knew, the mythology behind these strange tiny creatures came as a result of local tribal folklore to explain how and why some people in the community became wealthy all of a sudden.

Winona was not sure if such creatures actually existed, but she had met people who swore by them. Over the years, she had read newspaper stories about these creatures terrorizing their 'owners' or 'acquirers'. There was this particular Case she had read some years back . It was in The Chronicle of Bulawayo. It was a story about a man who had 'acquired' one of these tiny creatures from a *n'anga* [spirit medium]. The purpose of the acquisition was to become wealthy from his business franchises.

Initially he was happy as the creatures worked and made him amass great wealth. In return for their 'services' he fed them with 10kg of maize meal everyday. That was a simple enough requirement, so he didn't mind. Years passed. The man became famous; built a mansion in one of the posh suburbs in Bulawayo; owned a fleet of state-of-the-art cars; sent his kids to the most expensive and most sought after private schools; wined and dined in the most prestigious restaurants, hotels and social clubs; his wife wore the most exclusive *haute couture* bought straight from the Cat Walk

Runway of Milan, Paris, London, New York. Bottom line, he was enjoying the life!! Everyone admired him. Everyone marvelled at his wealth. Everyone wanted to be just like him. Parents used him as an example to their kids ... 'Work hard at school ... get good grades ... form your own businesses and become as successful as Goredema.' Five years down the line, the *sitokoloshi* started to demand more food ... more services ... 10kg was increased to 20kg per day ... then to 50kg ...

Culinary tastes became more sophisticated ... they changed from chicken to goat to a whole cow ... then finally to human flesh ...!! And mind you ... not just any human flesh ... but his children's ... The man was outraged and returned to his *n'anga* arguing and complaining that human flesh was never part of the original 'contractual' agreement.

There was no way he was going to agree on sacrificing his children!! The *n'anga* said there was nothing he could do to help the man. The creatures were well within their rights to ask for anything they wanted in return for their services. Goredema was furious and said

'In that case, take your creatures back!!'

To which the *n'anga* laughed and said

'Young man ... these creatures are non-returnable. When you acquired them, they came 'as is where is''

Goredema would not agree to it and replied

'NO!! I don't want them anymore!! Take your creatures back!!'

And with that he left the three creatures with the *n'anga* and stormed off in a huff and puff. To his nasty shock, when he got home, the three *sitokoloshi*s were already there ... at his home ... in their usual hiding place!!

Goredema was livid!! He gathered the creatures again and drove back to the *n'anga* and dumped them at his place. Again when he got home, he found that they had already come back to his home!! This time he went with them to the train station and tried to lure them so that they would be run over by the train.

Sure they had been run over, he rushed back home ... only to find ... yep ... you guessed right ... the three creatures were already back at his house!! Goredema was desperate!! Clearly he could not get rid of these creatures!! What was he going to do?!! Days passed ...

Then a thought hit him ... He decided to get rid of them once and for all ... He rushed back home ... called his creatures to him and started to play with them ... Seeing their owner 'happy' again, the creatures also relaxed and warmed up to their master.

When he was satisfied that he had successfully managed to lure them into a false sense of security, Goredema SWALLOWED THEM WHOLE !! Yes, you read right!!! ...He swallowed them whole !! ... all three of them!! Soon after that, Goredema started to walk ...

Initially he thought he was just taking a stroll to get rid of his sudden spring of energy ... That stroll turned into a run ... which soon turned into a sprint ...

When The Chronicle caught up with him a week later, he was still sprinting ...

A week had passed and he had been running nonstop, since ... He neither felt tired; nor stopped to rest; nor slept ...

Winona had shook her head as she recollected this story.

The things people got up to for wealth ... Aaaayaaa ...!! Now it looked like her client and the husband were involved in similar *n'anga* issues. She paced again

Chapter 7 - Hazel Jikinya

"Hazel Jikinya, is her name"

A familiar male voice said

"Heh ... ?"

Winona blinked She had just been woken up from a deep sleep by the shrieking of the phone on her side bed. She had reached for it without thinking

"The name of The Teacher-in-charge at St Gabriel Nursery when Tanatswa Nemapare went missing ..."

Chief Inspector Rapingwa filled in

"Oh, I see."

Winona's head was beginning to clear.

"Hazel Jikinya, you said?"

She clarified

"Yes."

Chief Inspector Rapingwa confirmed

"Great!"

Winona said as she sat up in her bed and reached for her Notebook. She jotted the name down.

"Would you by any chance have her physical address?"

Winona asked. Her little grey cells were now firing on all cylinders.

"The one registered in our files is ..."

There was a pause and a shuffling of papers ... then

"... 226 Jason Moyo Street, Charlottes Brooke, Harare."

Winona wrote frantically in her notebook.

"What about telephone or mobile number?"

Winona asked Again there was a pause on the other end, then

" ... 1891415141- 583 ..."

Again Winona scribbled in her notebook

"Great! Thank you!! I owe you one, Inspector!!"

Winona chuckled

"Yes. Dinner at The Ritz would do just nicely!!"

Chief Inspector Rapingwa chuckled back

"You got yourself a date!!"

Winona laughed Chief Inspector Rapingwa had helped her so many times over the years. He was like her partner.

"Great! I'll leave you now to enjoy your beauty sleep!!"

Chief Inspector Rapingwa laughed Winona glanced at the clock It was 6 in the morning!!

"Chief Inspector ... you drive a hard bargain ...!!"

She laughed

"Yeah, I know ... !!"

Chief Inspector Rapingwa laughed and disconnected the line. Winona was now fully awake. She glanced at her notes again ...

'Hazel Jikinya ... 226 Jason Moyo Street, Charlottes Brooke ... 1891415141 - 583 ...'

It was too early to call ... Winona decided to wake up, take a shower. Her Personal Chef, Chef Erica was preparing a special breakfast for her this morning.

Dinner was going to be for ten this evening as she was having guests over later. Chef Erica also had a special dinner lined up. Winona, Mrs Muterere and Chef Erica had discussed the menu at length over the past week. The Executive House Keeper, Mrs Muterere and her stuff were already busy cleaning the house.

Winona crept out of bed, slipped on her blue bedroom slippers and walked casually to her bathroom ... and my ... what a magnificent bathroom!! It had a huge marble bath tub, a jacuzzi, a separate shower with crystal partitions, crystal hand basins.

Her bathroom also boasted a state-of-the-art shower head, shower rose and beautiful curtains. After her shower and doing other ablutions, Winona wrapped herself with one of her navy blue towels, slipped into her slippers and paddled towards an adjoining door. It led to a Dressing Room ...fancy ... spacious ... lavish ...

It clearly was a HER Dressing Room. From her array of clothing and shoes, she selected what she was going to wear that day. She was planning on visiting Ms Hazel Jikinya. Charlottes Brooke was going to be a longish drive, so she decided to wear something comfortable.

She chose a pair of blue jeans and a light blue and white striped blouse. For her foot wear, she opted for comfortable light brown sandals. A pair of dangling pearl earrings completed the match. Winona then applied a light blue mascara over her eyelids, black eye liner; then finished it off with a deep rouge lipstick. She checked herself in the mirror and smiled.

Her day was just beginning.

"I am here to see Hazel Jikinya, please ..."

Winona announced. She had driven for over an hour to reach and find the woman's home. The guard by the gate said

"And who may I say is calling?"

"Winona Manyame ..."

Winona said She wilfully omitted to mention that she was a Private Investigator, just in case Hazel refused to see her off-hand.

"Ok. Wait here. I'll let her know."

The guard said and walked quickly towards the house. The house was double storey, painted light grey and black. It made for a stunning colour combination. Winona marvelled at the sheer size of it. Winona glanced this way and that whilst she waited. The neighbourhood also had impressive homes and landscaping.

Three to four cars per household could be seen parked along the driveway. Clearly Charlottes Brooke was a posh neighbourhood.A few minutes later she saw a woman approach. She was slim, light in complexion, tall ... Even from that distance, Winona could tell that she was a highly distinguished lady.

She was dressed in a casual floral skirt and plain blouse. On her feet, she had on a pair of sandals. The overall effect could only be described as stunning!! Winona smiled at the approaching woman.

"Hallo. I hear you are looking for Hazel Jikinya ...?"

The lady spoke

"Yes."

Winona replied

"That's me."

The lady smiled in a friendly way

"May I know who you are, please ...?!"

Hazel had an inquisitive look on her face

"My name is Winona Manyame. I am a Private Investigator."

Winona said, producing a card from her handbag and handing it over to Hazel. Hazel accepted the card and read through it.

"I am investigating a Case that happened ten years ago at the Nursery school you once worked for before it was shut down."

At this, Hazel's eyes became slits. She looked at Winona and said

"I remember the incident. It happened a long time ago. From what I remember, the Police carried out their investigation and could come out with no leads. The Nursery School in question was shut down after that. The Head was charged with negligence and served some time in prison. "

"Yes, I know. The reason I am contacting you is because the mother of the missing child has contracted me to re-open the investigation. Strange and mysterious things have been happening in her home."

Winona filled in

"I see. But I fail to see how any of this has anything to do with me ..."

Hazel trailed

"I understand from Chief Inspector Rapingwa that you were The Teacher-in-charge responsible for releasing the kids that day ..."

Winona spoke

"Yes, I was ..."

Hazel squinted her eyes even more

"Can you remember the description of the 'cousin' you released Tanatswa Nemapare to ...?"

Winona looked squarely at Hazel. The lady seemed to hesitate, then said

"But I already described the man to the police all those years ago ...?"

"I know. Still I want to hear it from the horse's mouth ..."

Winona produced a small smile. Hazel was quiet for a few seconds ... remembering

"He was short, dark, bold ... He was wearing a pair of navy green slacks and white sneakers ... I remember he stood with a stooper ... a sort of hump on his shoulders ... As I told the police back then, I had seen him a few times with Mr. Dambudzo as he picked up his kid."

Winona jotted in her notebook.

"I understand when Mr. Dambudzo was brought up for questioning, he said he had never brought anyone when he was picking up his kid ...?"

Winona looked at the other lady.

"That's what he said ... but I can swear I had seen that man before. That is why on the day in question, when the man came alone and requested for Tanatswa, I did not hesitate to hand her over to him."

Hazel filled in

"And what was the state of the child when you handed her over to the man?"

Winona looked at Hazel Hazel shrugged

"She looked happy enough ... I did not notice any sign of nervousness or withdrawal or anything like that ..."

Winona was clearly baffled. The crux of the matter revolved around Hazel, Dambudzo and the mysterious 'cousin' ... that she was sure. Either Hazel had been working in cohorts with the mysterious 'cousin' when the child disappeared or Dambudzo was lying about something...

How come Dambudzo 'forgot' to pick up his daughter on the day in question ... and the 'cousin' mysteriously pitched instead to pick up his kid? Could it have been a coincidence ...? Then another question hit her

"Did this happen often ... that Mr. Dambudzo would forget to pick up his kid from school sometimes ...?"

Winona fixed a stare at Hazel. To which the other lady shook her head vehemently and said

"NO!! Mr Dambudzo never forgot to pick up his kid, except on this fateful day."

Winona bit her bottom lip

'Interesting ...!!', she mused to herself

Hazel was also looking at her with the same curious look.

"You have been such a great help. Thank you for your time."

Winona smiled Hazel smiled back and said

"Glad to be of help ... I hope you find the child ..."

Winona nodded, turned and walked back to her SUV. A curious expression was on her face.

'Could we be looking at a Case of child smuggling here?'

Winona wondered

'Is it possible that Dambudzo, Hazel and this so-called 'cousin' were into child smuggling? Hmmm ...'

Winona got into her car ...

Chapter 8 - Reopen the Case

"Chief Inspector, didn't it strike you as odd at the time that Hazel Jikinya and Dambudzo Nemapare gave conflicting reports about the man in question who is said to have been the one who picked up Tanatswa that day? Clearly, either one of them is lying or they were working in cohorts. "

Winona was in Chief Inspector Rapingwa's office. She had passed by on her way from Hazel's home.

"Yes, we thought it odd and a conspiracy theory was suspected. The trouble was our investigation led us nowhere. "

Chief Inspector Rapingwa confessed

"Ok ... Say Dambudzo was working in cohorts with this mysterious 'cousin', what would he have to gain by having his own flesh and blood be kidnapped to the point of simply varnishing into thin air? No ransom demand was ever made."

Winona asked Chief Inspector Rapingwa paused a bit before answering

"That baffled us back then. One of our police officers working on the Case suggested 'for voodoo purposes ' ..."

Winona frowned

"I know it sounds crazy but that was the only logical explanation we could come up with. Unfortunately, the police force is not a place of superstitious mumbo-jumbo!! That explanation was dropped in the wastepaper basket. Here at The Police Force, we only work with facts ...and evidence!!"

Chief Inspector Rapingwa explained. Winona nodded. Ordinarily, she didn't believe in superstitious mumbo-jumbo either but her experience in her line of work had taught her never to dismiss any possible reason outright.

Basing on what she had just heard on the news, the possibility was there; ridiculous as it might seem. As a way to question his sentiment she said

"Did you hear about The *Nemapare Passenger Services* scandal? It was on the news a few days ago. "

Chief Inspector Rapingwa chuckled and said

"Yes, I saw it on the news. Apparently, passengers are now boycotting this Passenger Service believing it to be cursed!!"

"You realise, of course, that this Passenger Service belongs to Dambudzo and Ndakaripa Nemapare?"

Winona looked at the Chief Inspector.

"What?!!"

Chief Inspector Rapingwa jumped from his seat

"What do you mean?!! I didn't realise that The Nemapares are into the transportation business!! I only know of that restaurant ... *Munhira Grill* and the Fashion business ...!!"

"Chief Inspector, you are behind on your current news!! *Nemapare Passenger Services* belongs to Dambudzo and Ndakaripa ..."

Winona affirmed Chief Inspector Rapingwa produced a low whistle. He stood up and started to pace around

"I don't want to speak out of turn here, but it is possible that Dambudzo uses 'black magic' to get ahead in business ... "

Winona shrugged

"I have another theory ..."

She paused

"I'm all ears ..."

Chief Inspector Rapingwa favoured his friend with a penetrating stare. He really liked this girl!! Over the years, she had managed to solve some otherwise, difficult, 'dead' and 'buried' cases for his Police Force. She had a remarkable analytical brain ... saw things from a different perspective ...

"What if Hazel was working in cohorts with the mysterious 'cousin'? ... "

"Motive ...?"

Chief Inspector Rapingwa asked simply

"I don't know ... child racketeering ..."

Winona hazarded a guess

"Both possible reasons explain why a ransom was never asked. The child simply varnished into thin air!!"

Chief Inspector Rapingwa said

"I have a third possible scenario ..."

Chief Inspector Rapingwa volunteered

"Shoot ..."

Winona looked at her friend

"What if the three of them worked in cohorts ...?"

Chief Inspector Rapingwa spoke Winona's face brightened

"I thought of that ... Its possible ... The ploy to give conflicting reports could have been meant to confuse everyone and lift suspicion from any one of them ..."

Winona was now also pacing Chief Inspector Rapingwa's eyes gleamed. There was silence in the room as both friends ruminated on what they had just discussed.

"I think we need to reopen this Case ..."

Chief Inspector Rapingwa finally said

"I agree ..."

Winona said

"But where to start, is the question"

Chief Inspector Rapingwa swivelled in his chair reflectively.He was rearing to go. He knew his Team was rearing to go as well once they heard that they were reopening this Case. Police in Zimbabwe took the Case of the mysterious disappearance of children very seriously.

So did Child Protection Services. This organisation had been on their case for months after they failed to come up with any meaningful leads. They had criticised them brutally and mercilessly on the News.

Now it was his chance to exonerate himself and clear his conscience. This Case had bugged him for weeks after that. He could not eat, nor sleep

----

"Dinner was lovely"

A lady dressed in a black formal evening gown said. The ten invited guests were now enjoying their cocktails in one of the lounges

"Yes. The Chef outdid herself. My compliments to the chef!!"

Another man dressed in a formal evening three piece suit said.

"Linda ... Dennis ... you are too kind."

Winona smiled Linda and Dennis were a couple. Winona had worked with Dennis Nyathi on a number of Cases in the past, including the famous Jokwi Village Case the previous year. He was a Park Ranger and worked at Hwange National Park. She was proud of her Chef.

Once or twice in the month, she liked to showcase her personal chef's culinary skills. The ten were her regular guests. Over the years, they had come to realise that mid month and end of the month was Dinner at Winona's!! It was always a treat.

Five Star ... no ... Seven Star treatment !! And all for free!! Some couples had started using this time as Date Night!! Her personal Chef, Chef Erica, never stopped to amaze. No dish was ever served twice!! There was something always new at Winona's dinner table.

"She should open her own restaurant ..."

Another lady suggested

"If its Working Capital that she needs, I am here ..."

"Tendai, you are generous beyond measure. You can contact her directly. "

Winona laughed

"I already have ... TWICE!! And she says she is happy working for you!!"

Tendai scowled playfully

Winona laughed again

"I guess that means she is happy with you!! I don't know many chefs who can say that about their bosses ..."

Ezra chuckled and took a sip of his cocktail Ezra and Tendai were a couple Winona was friends with Ezra Gunguwo. Like Dennis, he was also a Park Ranger and they had worked together on a number of Cases including The Jokwi Village Case.

"Don't worry Tendai ... Right now she is producing a Book ..."

Winona highlighted

"A Cook Book, you mean?"

Linda sought clarification

"Yes ... a Cook Book ..."

Winona affirmed

"That's great!! At least she is not letting her talent go to waste!!"

Tendai smiled Winona smiled too. She moved on in the room, wielding her Mukai on the rocks. The ice crinkled in the crystal glass. The sugarcane juice with a touch of mint, ginger and lemon on top was utter divine.

"So, which Case are you working on these days?"

Ruramisai Nematumbai, ever the inquisitive one, asked

Winona smiled at her dear friend and said

"It's a ten year old Case ... You know the Client ..."

"Hmmm ...?!!"

Ruramisai quirked an eyebrow

"Yes. You recently referred her to me ..."

Winona smiled. Ruramisai frowned, trying to recollect. Winona continued with a twinkle in her eye

"Ndakaripa Nemapare ..."

"Oh, yes!!"

Ruramisai exclaimed

"I did!!"

She smiled in recollection. Then her expression changed. It became sombre

"It was a very sad Case. Happened ten years ago ... Nearly broke Ndakaripa's mental health ... She was actually institutionalized for a few months ... You see, she loved her daughter to the moon and back ..."

Winona gave her friend a serious look. Ruramisai frowned

"Strange how the husband denied ever knowing the man who came to pick up his kid ..."

"You think something fishy went on ...?"

Winona asked. Ruramisai sighed and confided

"I always thought there was more to his story than meets the eye ...I mean, how does he explain the coincidence that he 'forgets' to pick up his kid for the first time ever and bang, she gets picked up by some other 'strange' man and is never seen after that ...? !! Something does not add up ..."

Winona looked on Ruramisai was not yet done

"I think part of the reason Ndakaripa lost it was because she knew instinctively that her husband had something to do with their daughter's disappearance. The only thing was she could not prove it."

Winona listened on. She had a hunch. Ruramisai had more to get off her chest. Her hunch was right, for Ruramisai said

"The other strange thing is that, a few months after their child's disappearance, their businesses started to take off the ground at a meteoric rate."

"What's strange about that ...?"

Winona quizzed

"People talked ..."

Ruramisai shrugged. Winona frowned and said

"What do you mean 'people talked? Talked about what?!!"

She had a curious expression on her face. Ruramisai shrugged again, took a sip of her cocktail and said

"Well, they linked Tanatswa's disappearance with the 'success' of their businesses ..."

Ruramisai voiced

"Only, there was no proof ..."

Winona grappled at straws.

"There are some things you don't need proof for to prove that they are real, Winona ...You, of all people should know that by now ... what with the business you are in ...!!"

Ruramisai said. Winona was silent. She was thinking hard ...Guests mingled ...So did she. The night wore on ...

Chapter 9 - Chisi Walk

I think it's high time I spoke to Dambudzo, Winona thought. She lifted her telephone receiver and dialled. The phone rang once ... twice ... three times ... four ... still no answer. A few more rings and the phone went to voicemail.

Winona replaced the receiver back on its cradle. She would call later. Maybe he was in a Meeting or something like that, she reasoned with herself. She thought for a minute.

Winona decided to pay *Nemapare Passenger Services* a visit. Who knows, maybe she could get clues. She stood up, grabbed her coat, handbag, car keys, office keys and left her office, locking up behind her.

She breathed in deeply, felt her lungs fill up with the cool mid-afternoon air as was her habit every time she stepped outside and gazed up into the sky. Today was cloudy and on the chilly side ...

'8/8 cloud cover ...', she observed and mused to herself

She shivered slightly and clung to her jacket. Thankfully, she had worn a jacket and some knee length leather boots. She looked very feminine. She got out of the lift and rushed to her SUV. Five minutes later she was headed for the highway and then Chisipite, off Enterprise Road. The name Chisipite means 'overflowing spring'.

She decided to approach Chisipite Shopping Centre through Chisi Walk ... It was a scenic, garden route with perfectly manicured lawn, lush green trees and flowers ... past a Centre painted peach with a distinctive navy green roof ... The overall contrast to The Centre was stunning. Winona feasted her eyes on the house for a minute. Her eyes took on the peach wall and the navy green roof ...

'Stunning ...!!' she mumbled to herself

She focused on the road again and drove past. A few minutes later, she got into a gravel road ... glimpsed a navy green durawall up ahead, decided to turn right and spotted 'The Alley' sign right infront.

She drove past a garden shop that had flower samples embedded in oval shaped black ceramic pot plants. They were displayed beautifully outside. She drove past 'I Safari Outdoor Gear'

Driving on, Winona then veered left into a tarred road; spotted a cobalt blue car park in the distance. She then turned right and drove through past a gate into Chisipite Shopping Centre Bon Marche Parking Lot ... There, she saw loads of cars.

Deciding to continue on past a New & Used Cars Dealership, she spotted a Toyota Garage and Filling Station on her right. It was under renovation. Construction workers could be seen tinkering and hammering away at height, balancing rather precariously on timber scaffolding.

Winona, who was afraid of heights, felt dizzy watching the construction workers even though her feet were firmly planted on the ground. She had to shake her head once or twice to convince her mind that she was still on the ground and not at height!!

She breathed a sigh of relief when she noticed that to maintain safety, the construction workers had on white helmets, safety belts and safety shoes.

'At least ...!!', she thought

She drove on.

Two minutes later, a Vegetable Market enclosed by a plastered durawall could be seen up ahead. Immediately to the right, Bon Marche with its distinctive red rustic facebrick and eye catching flags could be spotted. Winona turned right and drove on past a chain of Fast Food Outlets ... Luger de Pollo ... Hafellis ... Chicken Inn ... Pizza Hut ... a bank, Cabs ... Thomson's ... Supreme ... Elegance ... Chisipite Post Office ... All these were visible to her on the left hand side.

As she continued on, she saw another vegetable market to her left hand side ... The specific stall that caught her attention was the one with a perfectly manicured thatched roof ... 'very distinctive and eye catching', she thought. She drove on ... saw Bolero up ahead then Bon Marche ... her final destination.

Bon Marche was a famous and one of the largest chain of supermarkets in Zimbabwe. It was a franchise. People loved this supermarket and drove long distances just to come and shop here because it offered fresh vegetables; an array of freshly baked bread, buns, hamburger rolls, meat pies; freshly baked cakes; good quality beef, tender chicken, an array of other red meat varieties such as mutton, liver, kidney, intestines ... the works!!

Yaive shara ude!!
[People were free to pick 'n' choose!!]

Besides offering these awesome foodstuffs, the supermarket also had a wing where it sold clothing items, shoes, electronics, stationary, school bags and so forth. It was a perfect One-Stop-Shop!!

Winona parked her SUV in one of the parking spaces, killed the engine, reached for her handbag and mobile phone that had been on the passenger seat, opened the door and got out. Locking the car behind, she walked in the direction of Bon Marche. *Nemapare Passenger Services* Headquarters was located on the first floor.

Winona spotted shoppers wheeling their trolleys around, topping up their groceries in the prestigious Bon Marche. As usual, it was full to the brim. Customers were milling about, enjoying their shopping escapade ... and yes ... shopping in Bon Marche was an experience and a half!!

Winona froze in her tracks as she looked longingly at the other customers, fighting the urge and temptation to go inside and indulge in one of her usual impulsive buying tendencies. However, she firmed her lips, put her shoulders back and walked on towards a lift up ahead. She pressed the button.

A yellow light popped on, indicating that it had 'heard' her 'call' to come and fetch her. Surely enough, twenty seconds later, the lift was on the ground floor and doors flew wide open. 'Open sesame!!!', Winona chuckled to herself, remembering a tale she had read once as a child in a book by Noboru Baba called 'Ali Baba and the Forty Thieves'

No one was inside the lift. She proceeded inside and pressed the button that would take her to the first floor. Doors closed and the lift propelled itself upwards. A few seconds later, the doors opened and Winona stepped out.

She was on the first floor alright. She looked about her with curiosity. Besides the Lobby, there were long corridors to the right and long corridors to the left. The long corridors had offices ... all clearly sign posted. She saw a sign written *'Nemapare Passenger Services'* to her left. She decided to follow the sign.

A long corridor lay sprawled infront of her. As she passed one office after another, she saw customers and clients waiting, seated by the lounge sofas in the waiting rooms ... clients talking to the Receptionist possibly making an appointment ... a Pharmacy ... a Driving Licence Agent ... a Parcel receiving and dispatch Agency ... a Multi-Speciality Clinic ... it was taking up quite a large space ... Winona walked on.

Nemapare Passenger Services was right at the end of the long corridor. The Double Glass Swing Door was open and a big sign '*Nemapare Passenger Services* ' was fixed right in front by the Shopfront. A couple of the sofas greeted one when they entered the office ... navy green ... leather ... The waiting area was to the left ... spacious ... Winona observed. A receptionist area was to the right, facing the waiting area. A young lady of about twenty something was on the phone.

"Yes. I'm afraid he cannot come to the phone right now. He is busy in a Meeting ..."

She spoke Her voice sounded beautiful, reassuring and light on the phone ...

'just as a Receptionist is supposed to sound!!', Winona observed

The Receptionist listened, then said

"Ok. I will tell him. Bye"

And replaced the receiver back on its cradle. She was dressed in a navy green and navy blue uniform. It was a three piece suit, complemented by a striped navy green, navy blue scarf. To say she looked smart, was a great understatement. She looked professional, all spruced up, all polished, all put together, in-control and in-charge.

A name tag with the same background colours indicated that her name was 'Penelope'. Winona smiled at the young Receptionist and introduced herself

"Hallo. My name is Winona Manyame. I am a Private Investigator."

With that she produced her business card and handed it over to the girl.

"I do not have an appointment, but I would like to see either Mrs Ndakaripa Nemapare or Mr. Dambudzo Nemapare ... if they are free, that is."

Winona kept her voice even. In truth, she actually wanted to see Dambudzo, but since she suspected that Dambudzo would not be that keen on receiving guests such as herself, bearing in mind the scandal that had occurred a week earlier, she decided to include Ndakaripa. A form of 'smokescreen', if you will. The Receptionist smiled and said

"May I know what this is in regard with, please?"

Winona remained friendly and said

"Oh, it's a personal matter. Mrs Ndakaripa Nemapare hired me"

There was nothing wrong with bending the truth, if only a little!!, Winona thought to herself Truth was, Ndakaripa was the one who had hired her and not her husband. For all she knew, possibly Ndakaripa hadn't informed her husband that she had hired a P.I

The girl smiled

"Oh, yes, Mrs Nemapare mentioned you!!"

An eagerness sprung on her face

"She said I could assist you with anything you needed ... anytime ..."

Winona was surprised at hearing this, but kept her poker face intact.

"Unfortunately, both Mr. and Mrs. Nemapare are not in the office right now. Is there anything I can assist you with?"

The girl flashed white, even teeth. She clearly felt at ease with the P.I lady!! Winona smiled and said

"Dan ... I really wanted to speak to either of them ...!!"

There is nothing like a little theatrics, Winona had learnt over the years in her line of business. She pretended to think for a minute ... then said

"Recently, I learnt on the news that your company had been accused of using voodoo to conduct business? Care to comment?"

Winona favoured the girl with a direct look. Penelope shifted uneasily in her seat. She looked right past Winona making sure there was not a listening ear. There was noone in The Waiting Room and noone coming through the doorway ...

'Coast clear ...!!', Winona mused to herself

Satisfied that they were quite alone, Penelope cleared her throat and said in a conspiratorial voice ....

"Actually about a third of my colleagues have resigned from the company as a result of the scandal and mysterious occurrences happening in the company ..."

Penelope began

"Really?!!"

Winona was all ears

"Tell me more ..."

Winona craned her neck to hear more ...

Chapter 10 - The distress Call

"Winona, you just have to come ..."

"Right now ...?!!"

Winona sat up in her bed She had been fast asleep She glanced at the clock on her bedside table. It was way past midnight!!

"Yes, RIGHT NOW!! It's happening again ...!! Come quick ...!!"

And the phone was disconnected Winona was left listening to a buzz on the line. She threw her sheets to one side and put her legs over the edge of the bed. As usual, her bedroom slippers were lying in wait for her by her bed in case she needed to get up during the night and use the washroom.

She slipped into them and thought for a minute. Clearly she had no other choice but to go!! She got up, walked briskly to her bathroom, opened the tap to one of her wash hand basins, sprinkled some cold water on her face to clear her head; then marched even more briskly to her Dressing Room.

There was no time for a shower!! She was in a hurry!! She quickly picked a pair of navy blue slacks, a matching tank top and white sneakers. She put them on; brushed her hair; applied some light Make Up.

She rummaged through her shoe rack and chose a pair of white sneakers. She then grabbed her handbag; mobile phone that had been charging on one of the tables in the bedroom; car keys and raced down the stairs. She was out of her bedroom so fast, one thought her house was on fire.

A beautiful chandelier flooded the whole balcony and stair area with light. Winona rushed to her front door; unlocked it, switched off the lights and walked out, firmly closing and locking the door behind her. Her yard was well lit.

She raced towards the garage, pressed a button and the Roller Shutter Door automatically opened. This time she walked to one of her sedans ... a top of the range car ... silver in colour. The garage housed eight cars. One look in her garage made you realise that Winona was a car fanatic ... vintages ... classic ... modern ... futuristic ... You name it, she had one of each.

The chosen car sprang to life, lights flicked on and she reversed out of the garage. The Roller Shutter Doors closed automatically as her luxury car purred on along the paved driveway. Perfectly manicured lawn ... fern trees ... rose bushes ... adorned the driveway. Clearly Winona had great taste and lived an elevated lifestyle.

The Security Guard in the cabin saw her approach, saluted and pressed a button to open the gate. He was used to seeing his boss pop in and out at the oddest of hours. He knew her line of business required her to do this once in a while. He smiled. Winona drove past, indicated to the left, made sure there was no oncoming traffic and pressed her leg on the gas pedal. Pretty soon she was driving on the highway heading for Glen Lorne. The road was deserted.

It was late after all. Forty five minutes later, Winona was slowing down, indicating to the right and cruising along a driveway. The main gate was located a few metres away. Perfectly manicured lawn throughout ... fern trees lining the driveway giving an avenues effect ... well lit ... it may just as well have been practically, daylight !! She drove on. Presently, she spotted a main gate right up ahead ...

A Security Guard came out of his cabin to investigate Winona pressed a button to open her window. She smiled

"Winona Manyame at your service ... I believe I am expected ...?"

And she produced her Driver's License for identification The Security guard took it and walked back to his cabin. Winona could hear him on his walkie-talkie ... A female voice came on ... He listened for a second ... And said

"Very well, Madam. I will let her in ..."

He pressed a button and the gate opened automatically. Winona drove right through ....

Bu ... bu ... bu ...
(Sound made by hands of a man clapping in a Shona traditional way)

"*Tisvikewo Mhukahuru* ...!!"
[Knock knock ...!!]

A 'gentleman' dressed in a three piece black suit, clapped his hands in a Shona traditional way as he stealthily entered the hut. There was a carefulness and cautiousness about him that was not characteristic of his usual manner. A man dressed in a most bizarre outfit sat cross legged inside. He had this distinctive *ngundu* [hat made of guinea fowl and peacock feathers].

His whole face had white paint marks, and what looked like *nyora* [scars that are deliberately put on the face by *n'angas* after infusing them with some kind of aryuvedic medicine].

The overall effect made him look like a *chinyau* [village warrior]. A long necklace made of sharp and vicious-looking crocodile teeth was draped around his neck. It hung from his neck and dangled all the way down to his entire chest. To add to his even more bizarre look, he was clad in a skirt made of feathers!! White, green and red beads hung around his wrists and ankles.

He was barefoot. *Iwo man'a*!!! [Talk about cracked heels!!] The strange looking man squinted his eyes as he saw someone enter his hut. Every one of his clients came by referral and appointment only. Made his rather sensitive and secret vocation easier to sustain.

He had been expecting this particular individual. His contact had informed him that the man was fed up of being broke all the time and was willing to do 'anything' to garner massive wealth ... and fast!! These were the clients *aaitsvaga nemaziso matsvuku*!! [Clients he salivated over!!]

In response to the greeting, the strange looking man nodded and motioned with his hand for the man to take a seat right in front of him. The 'seat' was a vacant area on the floor ... no mat ... no rug ... no carpet ... just bare earth.

The man sat down, mirroring the strange looking man. He sat cross legged. The hut was dark inside. A paraffin lamp lit the premises. Dark spirit face masks dangled around the place. Trinkets like bows, arrows, tsero, clay pots, human skulls, bones and feathers 'decorated' the whole place. Without wasting any time, the man said

'Muchiona ndasvika pano Mhukahuru, ndinoda rubatsiro kubva kwamuri ...' [The reason I am here is because I need your assistance, Sir ...]

The man kept on clapping his hands in that Shona traditional way as he spoke. The *n'anga* reached for his waist and produced a small brown cloth. It was tied at the edges. He unfolded it, revealing a brown substance & pinched a bit of it using his thumb and index finger. He directed the substance to one nostril, sniffed; then directed the substance to the other nostril and sniffed. A second later, he went

"Hotsiii ...!!"

He sneezed

"Svikai zvakanaka Mhukahuru ...!!"
Literal translation: [Arrive properly, Sir ...!!]
(A Shona traditional way of invoking spirits from the netherworld)

The man was clapping The *n'anga* retied his pouch and replaced it at his waist. His eyes were rolling in their eye sockets and he bellowed

"Ndiudze kuti unodei kwandiri ...!!"
[Tell me what you want me to do for you ...!!]

The man kept on clapping his hands in that traditional way

"Mhukahuru, muchiona ndasvikawo pano kudai, ndinoda rubatsiro kwamuri. Ndinonzwa kuti muri godobori hombe when it comes to kubatsira vanhu vakaita seni kuwana mari ..."
[Sir, I am here because I need some help from you. I understand that you are a guru when it comes to helping people like myself generate and amass huge sums of wealth]

"You heard right ..." The *n'anga* spoke in that deep voice

He then reached for his *hakata* [traditional instruments that he uses to communicate with the oracles] and threw them on the floor.

"Hiirii hiirii ...!!"

He produced an odd sound with his tongue. The man kept on clappingHis gaze was now fixed on the *hakata* that had scattered on the ground. He was trying to make head or tail of them. Of course, that was a futile exercise ...!! It was like someone trying to read their palm when they know next to nothing about palm reading!! The *n'anga* too, was gazing at his instruments.

For him it was like someone looking at his pair of compasses. He could read the coordinates very well and what they meant.

"I see here that you and your wife have been trying to generate wealth for years, to no avail ...?"

The *n'anga* said

"Yes ..."

The man replied. He was now sitting up with an alert expression on his face. He was still gazing at the *hakata*. The *n'anga* raised his head and stared squarely at the man.

"Be warned ...What you want me to do for you will cost you ... not in terms of money, but in terms of sacrifice ..."

"Name it ..."

The man said without blinking an eye. He was ready for anything. Whatever it took, he was willing to do it. Poverty be damned!!

"Good ..."

The *n'anga* smiled ... no ... he more of snarled ... A dark ugly look had sprung into his eyes ...

Chapter 11 – Listen

"Come in, Winona ... Glad you could make it at such short notice ..."

Ndakaripa said as she ushered Winona inside her house

"It was the least I could do ... You sounded so distraught on the phone ... What is the matter?!!"

Winona shivered as she stepped inside her client's home. There was something strange about the house ... It felt eerie ... dark ... menacing ... dangerous ... Again, Winona shivered Ndakaripa led her straight along the corridor. It was well lit ... spacious ...

"Listen ..."

She whispered Winona was very still. At first she could not hear anything ... She remained still ... Ndakaripa was holding her left hand; very firmly, as if for support. Winona kept very still ... She listened ... Then she heard footsteps ... a peter-pater of footsteps ... It sounded like the one made by a girl child wearing baby shoes ... She tensed ... Where was the sound coming from ...? She wheeled around ...

There was laughter ... no ... giggling ... It was a chuckle of a little girl ...the sound a girl normally makes when she is playing with someone and having fun ... Common sense hitting her, Winona opened her handbag and produced her tape recorder. Thank goodness she had remembered to bring it along. In her line of work, it was something she used often.

She pressed the 'RECORD' button. The footsteps and cheerful laughter continued ... Ndakaripa was also listening intently ... After about two minutes, the footsteps moved ... They were going in the direction of a room ... It had been closed ...

Winona and Ndakaripa followed ... Ndakaripa opened the door and switched on the lights ... It was a little girl's bedroom ... Very beautiful ... baby pink was the overall theme ... a beautifully made bed ... a wardrobe ... a reading space adorned with a bookshelf and lots of books ... a table beneath ... white lace curtains ... As Winona looked around, she realized, much to her surprise, that this was a shrine ...

She looked at Ndakaripa for clarification, but Ndakaripa was looking on the tiled floor ... She was listening intently. Winona listened too ...

'Mummy ... mummy ... come tuck me in ... I am tired now. I want to sleep ...'

The little girl's voice said Winona looked around but could not see the person who had just spoken. She gave a questioning glance towards Ndakaripa but Ndakaripa was now leaning over the bed.

The duvet cover moved of its own volition ... Winona saw the sheets crinkle like someone was lying on them. She gasped and looked at Ndakaripa again. This time Ndakaripa was folding back the duvet cover as if she was covering someone with it. A contented sigh emanated from the sheets. Ndakaripa said

"Sleep well my darling ..."

She paused to take a look at the bed, turned and walked towards the door. Winona followed. She could not believe what she had just witnessed She felt like she had just watched one of those 'Hammer House of Horror' movies!!

After making sure Winona was back in the well-lit corridor, Ndakaripa switched off the lights in the bedroom and closed the door quietly behind her. She then walked in the direction in which they had come from; only this time, she led her towards a lounge. It was a bit of a distance from the bedroom.

Ndakaripa ushered Winona to one of the couches. Winona thankfully sat down. Ndakaripa sat opposite Winona. The two women were silent ... Both were ruminating on what they had just witnessed. Winona switched off the tape recorder. She stared at it.

What had just happened? Who was that little girl and how come they could not see her yet hear her? Clearly the little girl was very much present in this house ... And Ndakaripa had tucked her into bed ...?!! Winona flinched. This was spooky at the least and satanic at the worst!! What was happening in this house?

Clearly Ndakaripa had some explaining to do. And where was Dambudzo? And the other child? This and more are the questions that hounded Winona as she sat facing her client. A few minutes passed ... then Ndakaripa said

"I am sure you have a lot of questions ..."

Winona remained silent. She just stared at her Client

'Who was this woman and what had she and her husband done?'

Winona grimaced. Ndakaripa winced when she saw the disturbed look in Winona's eyes. She looked almost revolted. She braced herself and continued

"For example, what just happened ...?"

Winona nodded Words were failing her.

"What you just witnessed is the footsteps of my little daughter ... Tanatswa. The peter-pater of steps you heard are caused by the shoes she had been wearing on the day she disappeared."

Ndakaripa began

"The episode you just witnessed has been repeating itself every two weeks exactly a year after Tanatswa disappeared."

Ndakaripa stopped

"I ... I heard her voice ... She spoke to you ... Asked you to tuck her in ..."

Winona's head was spinning. She could hardly believe what she had just seen and heard

"Yes ..."

Ndakaripa replied simply

"But ... but that doesn't make any sense ... !! Your little girl disappeared ten years ago, yet she is very much present in this house...?!! How can that be?"

Winona stared at Ndakaripa's face, hoping to find some answers

"That's just it !! I don't know. That's what I was trying to explain to you when we first met that day at the restaurant ..."

Ndakaripa spoke. Winona stood up. Her little grey cells were now working overtime. She began pacing

"There is something we are missing here ..."

Winona voiced

"What could it be?"

Ndakaripa looked just as frustrated Winona frowned

"Tanatswa disappeared when she was five. You are contacting me ten years later; meaning Tanatswa should be fifteen by now. How come she is still a little girl ...? She seems to be trapped in a five year old body ... How come?"

Ndakaripa frowned as well

"It baffles me too ..."

Then as a thought suddenly flashed into her mind, Winona stopped in her tracks, whirled to face her Client and said

"Wait ...!! You bought and moved into this house a few years AFTER Tanatswa disappeared ... right?"

Winona asked, biting her bottom lip

"Yes. Why?"

Ndakaripa said

"How come your little girl is present HERE, in THIS house?!!"

Winona mulled her bottom lip

"What are you trying to get at?"

Ndakaripa looked confused

"I am thinking ... if your little girl disappeared BEFORE you came to live in this house, then she should not be present in THIS house. It would make sense if she was present in your old house, not this one!!"

Winona reasoned. Ndakaripa stood up and started pacing as well. What Winona was saying made sense. She had not thought of it that way before. Winona winced as she braced herself for what she was about to say next. She did not want to hurt Ndakaripa unnecessarily but she knew that the sooner she faced a possible reality, the better she could move on with her life. She cleared her throat

"Ndakaripa you realise something else ...?"

"What?"

Ndakaripa looked at Winona

"Have you considered the fact that Tanatswa appearing here in this house, means her SPIRIT is here ...?!!

This further means she is possibly gone ... passed on ..."

Winona tried to break this to her as gently as she could. She didn't want Ndakaripa to fall to pieces.

"Yes, I have considered that possibility ..."

Ndakaripa trailed. Winona breathed. She heaved a sigh of relief. At least Ndakaripa was being brave, practical and realistic in all this. This made her investigation into this Case that much easier.

"I have another question ..."

Winona continued

"Earlier I noticed that you have a designated bedroom for Tanatswa ...? Why is that? I would have thought that since you moved into this new house AFTER her disappearance, you would not have a special bedroom for her?"

Winona trailed. Ndakaripa was silent for a minute. She was wrestling with her mind, then said

"When we moved here, I was still hopeful that our little girl would be found. So I insisted we reserve a room for her. Dambudzo resisted at first. But he only came around after I threatened to leave him if he didn't allow me to do this one thing for our little girl. So he agreed."

Ndakaripa explained. Winona nodded. That made sense. One could not blame a mother for still continuing to hope that her baby would be found.

"Talking about your better half, where is your husband tonight?"

Winona asked

"Dambudzo ... he is out of town on business. "

Ndakaripa blinked

"OK. During our first meeting, I seem to remember you said you and your husband have another child ...?"

Winona hesitated

"Yes ... Tanaka ... He is sleeping over at a friend's house ... birthday party ..."

Ndakaripa supplied

"Tanaka should be thirteen by now ...?"

Winona paused, seeking clarification

"Yes ... twelve and a half. He will turn thirteen in about a month"

Ndakaripa's face softened. It was clear Ndakaripa loved her children very much. Winona could not imagine Ndakaripa purposely harming any of her children. She relaxed a bit

"Ok. And you said these mysterious occurrences have been happening regularly ... by your count ... every two weeks starting exactly a year after Tanatswa's disappearance?"

Winona sought clarification

"Yes"

Ndakaripa nodded

"And you said your husband dismissed them ...?"

Winona paused

"Yes ... He says he doesn't hear anything and that it must be a figment of my own over-heightened imagination."

That look of desperation was back on Ndakaripa's face again

"In that case, I have an over-heightened imagination as well; for I just heard the footsteps and the voice of a little girl ..."

Winona frowned. What was going on? Why was the husband denying what clearly anyone with two ears and eyes could see? Did he know something we did not ...? Winona paced again

"You are the first person I have allowed inside the house when this is happening ... and that's because Dambudzo is away; otherwise, he would have forbade me to call you ..."

Ndakaripa revealed

"Ummm ..."

Winona said again. What was this man afraid of? What did he know about the mysterious disappearance of his daughter that they didn't?!! Winona thought to herself and paced again

"Tanaka ... does he hear the sounds too?"

Winona asked

"Yes. Sometimes I hear him playing with his sister in her room ... calling her by name ..."

Ndakaripa confessed

"To which Dambudzo gets really mad and shouts at me for influencing our son ..."

Ndakaripa had a sad look

"I see"

Winona said. Then as a thought hit her she suddenly stopped pacing and said

"Have you thought of exorcism?"

A shoe could have dropped. There was total silence. As if that was not enough, there was a long pause from Ndakaripa. She seemed to be struggling to come up with the right words. Winona watched her closely. She watched the play of emotions flicker on her face. Then seeming to have come to a decision, she said

"Dambudzo does not believe in that religious mumbo-jumbo! He says it's fake"

Clearly there was a problem in this house and Dambudzo sat right in the middle of it!! Winona felt furious!!

'Wait till I get my hands on this man ...!!'

She fumed

'I will make him regret the day he was born!!'

Winona made a fist and snarled. She felt like punching Dambudzo. He was using bullying tactics to subjugate his wife and get his way. Ndakaripa was way too subservient.

Winona continued pacing again ...What could she do, Winona agonised with herself. She needed to think ... She needed a strategy ...She stopped pacing and sat down. She glanced at her watch ...It was way past the bewitching hour ...

Chapter 12 - The Deal

"Most people hesitate when they hear what I suggest for them to sacrifice ... but I think you are different ... you look like you want wealth badly enough ...?"

The *n'anga* favoured the man with a fixed stare. The stare was ugly, dark and penetrating. The man shivered, but held the stare. The *n'anga* went

"*Hoootsiii* ... !!"

Again the man said

"*Svikai zvakanaka Mhukahuru ...!!*"

And started clapping again in that Shona traditional way

"Alright ...”

Reaching into a clay pot behind him which the man had failed to spot when he first got inside the hut, the *n'anga* produced a black soiled cloth; dusted it theatrically and blew on it. He then untied it. The man saw five sticks ... dry ... They were the size of fingers ...

The *n'anga* examined the five sticks closely, then chose one particular one. It was the longest of the five, on the deformed side. He placed the stick on the floor next to the *hakata*; tied the cloth and replaced it carefully inside the clay pot. He turned and took the stick. He gave it to the man, saying

"Take this and go home with it. Place the stick where no one is likely to find it ... not even your wife. In five days' time, your sacrifice will be ready. Come back then. You will not need to bring the stick back with you. It would have returned to me on its own accord along with your sacrifice"

To which the man grinned and accepted the stick eagerly. He put it in his top left shirt pocket and proceeded to clap in that Shona traditional way.

"For my services, I will ask for you to bring me a female black goat - a kid, not more than six months old ... a *jongwe* [cock] ... again black in colour ... a *sheche* [a hen], white in colour ... The moment you bring me these, I will consider it as our Contract having been agreed. There will be no turning back from here."

Again, the *n'anga* favoured the man with that penetrating stare

"Think carefully before you bring these items to me; for there will be no turning back after that."

But the man did not have to think twice ... He had thought long and hard about this and his mind was made up. So he calmly said

"I'll have your payment by tomorrow evening"

The *n'anga* looked satisfied. There was something about this man that he liked. Unlike most of his clients, this one knew exactly what he wanted and he wasn't backing down. He liked and admired that!!

'Man with a backbone.'

He muttered to himself with deep satisfaction If he played his cards right, this client was the one who was going to bring him a huge fortune!! That double storey mansion he was building in Marlborough would be finished within the year!! Then he would start on that commercial farm project. Hmmm ... life was looking up, he snarled

The man left, still clapping in that Shona traditional way.

True to his word, the following day the man brought the requested items. A 'gentleman's agreement' had just been 'signed' There was no going back now.

"Good!!"

The *n'anga* smiled. Now he had this man right where he wanted him ... 'hook, line and sinker'!!

'Marlborough here we come!!'

The *n'anga* grinned

"Did you put the stick somewhere safe, where no one will spot or touch it?"

The *n'anga* stared at the man

"Yes"

The man smiled

"Good!!"

The *n'anga* gave a satisfied look

"Come back in four days. Your sacrificial lamb will be ready by then"

The man grinned and nodded Wealth, here we come!!, he thought. He felt like break dancing!! He was on cloud nine!! No more scrounging every month to make ends meet!! No more quarrelling with the wife about money!! No more bickering with the landlord about rent!! Hell, if all goes well, he will be so wealthy enough to finish building The Malborough mansion then go onto buy another mansion in Borrowdale Brooke ... !!

Life was looking up!! Finally!!, he grinned to himself

'And they say this type of business does not pay?!!'

The *n'anga* sniffed. As he was about to go through the doorway, the *n'anga* seemed to have a final thought ...

"Oh, and by the way, on Friday, don't pick up your daughter from school ..."

The man stopped and veered back

"What?!!"

He frowned. He looked confused, apprehensive all of a sudden

"Yes, you heard me ... Someone else will ..."

The *n'anga* turned and gave his back to the man. The man shuddered. What had he done?!!!

"That sounds like a little girl's voice and those footsteps, they sound eerie!!"

Chief Inspector Rapingwa frowned

"Yes, that little girl's voice belongs to Tanatswa ..."

Winona frowned at The Chief Inspector. Chief Inspector Rapingwa gave Winona a sharp look

"You mean Tanatswa Nemapare?!! Where is she?!! Have you found her?"

There was an urgency in his voice Winona remained silent for a minute. She knew that what she was about to say would sound controversial and if she didn't present the facts she had gathered so far well, Chief Inspector

Rapingwa was likely to throw her and her tape recorder out of his office and into the street!!

Chief Inspector Rapingwa was a policeman; not a priest!!

"Yes, the voice and footsteps that you just heard on the recorder do belong to Tanatswa Nemapare. She was five years old then ... I taped her last night when her mother summoned me to her home in distress."

Winona began

"Wait a minute ... let me get this straight ... You say you taped her last night at her parents' home ... but it can't be because Tanatswa should be about fourteen now by my count ... not five ...?"

Chief Inspector Rapingwa frowned

"Fifteen to be exact."

Winona corrected

"Yes. So, how can she be five when you tape recorded her last night ...?!!"

Chief Inspector Rapingwa was looking at Winona like she had lost her senses

"That's just it, Chief Inspector. Had I not witnessed it with my own eyes, I'd have asked the exact same question you are asking me now."

Winona shifted uncomfortably in her seat.

"Fact is, when I got to Ndakaripa's house last night, she immediately let me in. She directed me towards the corridor ... that's where you heard the footsteps ... A few minutes later, the footsteps started towards a bedroom ... We followed. Ndakaripa opened the door and switched on the light. The voice of a little girl you just heard on the recorder is the sound of the same little girl. She referred to Ndakaripa as 'mummy' I saw the duvet move to one side as if someone had flicked it ... then I saw the sheets move as if a weight had gotten on top of it.

Ndakaripa walked over and tucked the bed just as the little girl had requested. That is when the little girl produced that contented sigh you just heard."

Winona finished Chief Inspector Rapingwa was silent for a full minute. What Winona was implying was that Ndakaripa and Dambudzo's home was haunted!! And it was haunted, not just by any spirit, but by their little girl's spirit!!

'Goodness!!', he exclaimed to himself; stood up and started pacing.

He really needed a smoke just then!! He had not smoked in years ... had never craved for it since he quit more than ten years ago ... not until now!!

His right hand shook. He was nervous all of a sudden. What he was looking at, was the case of the supernatural!! If what Winona was saying was indeed true, then it meant that Tanatswa was dead and her spirit was caught in that house ...!!

He then linked the Passenger Services incident with the goings-on at the home. He broke a sweat on his forehead ...

'How were they going to tackle this Case from here onward ...?', he cringed

He stopped his pacing, came back to take his seat facing Winona and said

"Boy, what are we going to do ...?!!"

Winona looked at him.

"I suggest you re-open the Case ...Since the spirit of the little girl is roaming inside the house, my hunch says her body is buried somewhere around the home ... "

Winona paused

"...the garden, perhaps ...?"

Chief Inspector Rapingwa hazarded a guess

"Maybe ..."

Winona bit her bottom lip

But Chief Inspector Rapingwa had another thought

"But how can her body be buried somewhere around the home when Tanatswa disappeared years BEFORE the family bought and moved into this house?!!"

"Excellent question ..."

Winona frowned

"Logically one would think that if Tanatswa was killed, she would have had been killed during the time the family was staying at their old house and if any burying had to be done, then it would have been carried out at their old house ..."

Winona trailed

"True ..."

Chief Inspector Rapingwa trailed as well. Winona shrugged and said

"In that case, it means we will have to look for her body in BOTH homes then ..."

Chief Inspector Rapingwa stared at Winona. The woman made a whole lot of sense ... !!!

"You have no right to be here ...!!"

Dambudzo shouted He had just woken up only to find the police everywhere. More than twelve police vans were parked around his yard. He could spot various teams placed all over his garden ... They were busy digging ...

"My name is Chief Inspector Rapingwa of Harare Precinct."

He said displaying his badge

"I have a Search Warrant."

Again he displayed an A4 Paper he produced from his shirt pocket

"We have reason to believe that a body may be buried here"

"Body ... buried here ...?!! What are you talking about?!! Whose body?!!"

Dambudzo panicked

"Mr. Nemapare, we have reopened the Case of the disappearance of your daughter, Tanatswa."

Chief Inspector Rapingwa informed

"What?!! Tanatswa ...?!! But that Case was closed ten years ago!! I thought you closed it because you could not get any leads as to what happened to my daughter?!! Why are you opening it again?"

Dambudzo rubbed his hair in a gesture of frustration and confusion. A lady he had not noticed before until then suddenly appeared. She was tall ... beautiful ...

"Mr Nemapare, my name is Winona Manyame. I am a Private Investigator. Your wife hired me to investigate the mysterious disappearance of your little girl ten years ago"

She said producing her business card

"What?!!"

Dambudzo frowned taking a quick glance at the business card

"Ndakaripa never told me this!!"

"I am not surprised bearing in mind the way you keep on refusing to discuss the strange, mysterious occurrences that have been happening in your house for the last nine years ..."

Winona spoke

"What 'strange and mysterious occurrences'?!!"

Dambudzo produced a dark look

"The mysterious footsteps and voices of a little girl that can be heard by your wife in your house roughly every fortnight, for instance."

Chief Inspector Rapingwa came straight to the point

"I have no idea what you are talking about!!"

Dambudzo swallowed

"My wife is delusional!!"

"In that case, so am I, Mr. Nemapare!!"

Winona had a rueful look on her face

"What do you mean?!!"

Dambudzo cringed

"What she means is, she heard the footsteps and voices as well, a few days ago when she rushed to your home after receiving a distress call from your wife."

Chief Inspector Rapingwa clarified

"Had Ms Manyame here not had the presence of mind to record what she heard, I'd have thought her looney as well "

Dambudzo breathed. He rubbed his hand again over his head. He could not believe what was happening. And where was Ndakaripa?!!, he thought furiously. His blasted wife had dared disobey him and do things behind his back!! He would have a thing or two to say to her when next he saw her!!

Ordinarily he did not believe in lifting a hand to hit his wife, but as he stood there fuming, he was seriously considering it. Thanks to her she was about to put everything in jeopardy!! How dare she!! Just then, Ndakaripa came out of the house accompanied by a woman who was wearing plain clothes.

Upon closer inspection, Dambudzo noticed that she had around her neck a badge that read: 'Erica M. Machiwenyika - Child Protection Services'. She was saying

"Yes. Feel free to search the whole house, Ms Machiwenyika ..."

'Child Protection Services ...?!!'

Dambudzo squirmed

'Dan ...!!'

Their presence spelt trouble, that he was sure. They had zero tolerance for any parent who mistreated their child. Fear, anxiety, anger, confusion made Dambudzo lash out. He sprung at his wife and said

"What is all this, Ndakaripa?!! Why are all these Police and Child Protection Services people here?!!"

And without waiting for her to reply continued

"And I just received a phone call from our tenant staying at our old home ... Gladys Mpofu. She was fuming and screaming obscenities at me saying that the police are all over the premises digging looking for a so called body ...!!"

Ndakaripa stopped and looked towards her husband. She was totally calm

"I trust you have met Chief Inspector Rapingwa and Ms Winona Manyame here ...?"

She spoke slowly, deliberately

"Yes!! Yes!!"

Unlike his wife, Dambudzo's voice was far from being calm

"My question to you is, what are they doing here?!! Why didn't you discuss this with me first?!!"

Ndakaripa looked bored and irritated

"Let's not do this right now, Dambudzo. Let the Police and Child Protection Services do their job. They are here under my instigation."

Ndakaripa said and turned her back to say something softly to Erica. Feeling totally disrespected, Dambudzo whirled around and marched around his yard. There were police everywhere ... digging ... searching ... Alsatians ... sniffing ... This intrusion had happened without prior notice. Dambudzo was nervous.

Hanzi kuvhunduka chati kwatara hunge uine katurike!!
[Literal translation: Those who panic at the sound of a slight noise are the ones with something to hide]

'Damn, Ndakaripa!!'

Things were likely to turn upside down ...!! He looked around nervously. He needed to get away from here ... He fiddled with his pant pockets ... He needed to consult ... and fast ... Dambudzo reached into his pants pocket and produced a set of car keys ... Before anyone knew what was happening, he could be seen driving away at full speed ... Winona, Chief Inspector Rapingwa and Ndakaripa watched him leave ...

'I wonder where he is rushing off to at such great speed ...?!!'

Winona mused. The glint in Chief Inspector Rapingwa's eyes told Winona that he had the same thoughts on his mind. Ndakaripa had a far away expression on her face ...

Chapter 13 - The Sacrifice

"Your sacrifice is already here ..."

The *n'anga* grinned. The man gingerly stepped inside the hut. A sack tied to the edge lay on the floor beside the *n'anga*. As the man sat cross legged to face the *n'anga*, the contents of the sack moved.

Someone was wriggling inside. A muffled voice could be heard. Another man he had not seen before was standing in the shadows. He stood with a stooper. He was a hunchback. When the sack started moving, he had automatically reached for it and said roughly

"Quiet!!"

Then added in a threatening manner

"Or do you want a repeat of what I did to you just an hour ago?!!"

To which the wriggling instantly stopped. The man corked his head. Had that been the muffled sound of a little girl's voice?, he asked himself. The voice had sounded rather familiar, he frowned. He looked towards the man who had just spoken.

When the hunchback had emerged briefly into the light, the man had noticed that he was short, dark, bold ... He was wearing a pair of navy green slacks and white sneakers ...The man had looked at the sack again. It had stopped moving.

"My sacrifice, *Mhukahuru*?"

The man shifted uncomfortably in his tracks

"May I know what it is?"

He swallowed. At the sound of his voice, the sack wriggled again; this time more frantically. The muffled voice became louder The man could swear the sound that emanated from the sack said ...

'Daddy ... help ...!!'

Could that be ... ?!! The man shook his head vigorously. No, it couldn't be ...!! Not his little ...

"Just keep your head, Mister!!"

The *n'anga* warned

"Everything is coming out as planned. All you need to do now is wait a few minutes whilst Ripai here gets to work. You will have your sacrifice in a package "

"'Package' ...?!!"

The man frowned, looking first at the sack, then the mysterious hunchback and lastly, the *n'anga*. The hunchback looked at the *n'anga*, who nodded in silent affirmation. The hunchback walked over to the sack and lifted it with ease. He placed the weight on his left shoulder and started to walk out of the hut. Whoever or whatever was in the sack, started wriggling again.

The hunchback held it fast so that it would not drop to the ground. He was out of the hut for twenty minutes flat. This time, when he marched back inside the rather dark hut he had with him a much smaller package ... the size of a shoe box. He handed the 'package' over to the *n'anga*; who took it and placed it on the floor between them.

The man watched the 'package' like it would spring to life. He looked fearful. His mouth felt dry. He was breathing fast. The *n'anga* then proceeded to throw his *hakata* on the floor, to which they scattered making a rickety sound. He sniffed his tobacco; sneezed and said

"It's all done now ...!!"

Then sprinkled some of his tobacco on the 'package' that was now covered with a black cotton cloth and tied around at the edges.

"Hotsiii .. !!"

He sneezed again. This time the man was too distraught and disturbed by what had just transpired to remember to clap in the Shona traditional way. Instead, he just stared at the 'package'. What was inside? Instinctively he knew what was inside, but at this stage he preferred to 'hide his head in the sand, ostrich-like', and pretend like he did not know. Funny what the mind can convince itself!! How was he going to live with himself after this?, he agonised

"Here. Take it. Keep it in the deep freeze, away from the prying eyes of your wife and house help. Is that clear?"

The *n'anga* favoured him with a fixed stare. His eyes were blood shot; his hands rough ... like he tilled the land a lot.

"Crystal ...!!"

The man said accepting the 'package'. His hands trembled. The 'package' felt oddly heavy. He stumbled out of the hut ... The *n'anga* licked his lips *samaserwe* [a type of house snake] The hunchback grinned.

"Ok, off you go!! Back in your place ..."

The *n'anga* said motioning to the clay pot. The hunchback suddenly disappeared ... and in his place, a 'stick' lay on the ground. The *n'anga* snarled, reached over and picked up the 'stick' ; opened the clay pot and dropped the 'stick' inside. He rubbed his hands in an anticipatory way and grinned ... The Plan with a capital P was now underway ... It was now in full swing ...

There was no going back now ...

Chapter 14 - Dambudzo is at it again!!

"Winona, you've got to come!! Dambudzo is at it again ... Please hurry ...!! We are at home ...!!"

And the line was disconnected Winona sat up in her bed abruptly She had been fast asleep. She glanced at her bedside clock. It had gone past midnight. Her mind cleared. She had to hurry!! Ndakaripa needed her!! And what did she mean when she had said 'Dambudzo was at it again ...!!' She jumped from her bed and ran to her dresser. She does not remember what she had put on. Five minutes later she was racing towards Glen Lorne.

"He is in here!! ..."

Ndakaripa was beside herself with worry. She ushered Winona into the main bedroom upstairs. The scene that confronted Winona was like none she had ever seen before. A man, about 6 foot something, dressed in a pair of matching pyjamas, was lying sprawled on the floor. He was gasping for breath. Froth was coming from his mouth. It looked like he was having difficulty breathing.

"Is he epileptic?!!"

Winona shouted above the gagging sound the man was making.

"No!!"

Ndakaripa shouted back

"Then what's happening to him?!! What happened?!!"

Winona tried to help the man up, but he wriggled his hand and seemed to shrink from her.

"He is having one of his anxiety attacks."

Ndakaripa looked at her husband. A helpless expression was mirrored on her face.

"Shouldn't we call an ambulance?!! He looks to be in pretty bad shape to me."

Winona asked, automatically reaching for her mobile. But Ndakaripa shook her head

"He doesn't want me to ..."

"What do you mean 'he doesn't want you to?!!' That's preposterous!! He needs medical attention ... and fast!!"

Ignoring Ndakaripa's protests, Winona dialled

"We need an ambulance right away!! Yes A man is having a seizure ... Hurry !!! ... The address ... yes ... its 328 Gumbo Road, Glen Lorne ... Thank you ... Please hurry ...!!"

And Winona disconnected the line. The man who had been wriggling and crying out in agony now wriggled even more. This time the moaning and groaning had stopped. His eyes rolled in their sockets and he wriggled one more time before his whole body went limp. The body looked contorted and he went into a coma.

"My goodness ...!!"

Winona was now beside herself with worry

"Now what do we do ?!! ... And where is that ambulance?!!", she screamed
Ndakaripa was now weeping silently.

All of a sudden, they heard sirens ... The ambulance was coming ...Winona
ran to the door and raced downstairs, into the lobby and out through the
main front door. She could spot cobalt blue lights a few metres away ...
They were flashing and flicking. Obviously the medical personnel were
liaising with the security guard.

Presently the gate opened automatically ... The ambulance sped inside the
yard ... Winona waved. The ambulance stopped in front of the main front
door under the bulkhead. Doors were flung wide open as the ambulance
personnel brought out a stretcher bed and wheeled it swiftly inside the
house.

"This way ..."

Winona led the way. The medical team followed. Winona rushed upstairs.
The medical team folded the stretcher bed and pursued Winona. The man
was still lying motionless on the floor. Ndakaripa was beside him, holding his
limp hand. It looked like he was not breathing. The medical team did not
need any further prompting. They set to work.

"What happened?"

One of the Medical personnel asked. Despite having sprinted two flights of
stairs, she sounded surprisingly calm. I guess they are used to doing this
kind of physical exertion in their line of work, Winona thought

"We had just finished having ... having ... "

Ndakaripa gagged. She looked embarrassed

"You mean, you had just finished having 'matrimonial relations' with your husband, when he got into this state?"

The lady suggested helpfully. Ndakaripa only nodded

"Has this happened before?"

The lady asked, jotting frantically in her notebook Again, Ndakaripa nodded

"Hmmmm ..."

The lady said. As Ndakaripa and the Medical lady spoke, the other two men were examining the man. Five minutes later they had checked the man's vitals, attached a drip in his veins and propped him onto the stretcher bed. They carried the stretcher bed with the man securely braced around it and carefully walked down the stairs.

Two minutes later, they were carefully placing the now distended bed into the back of the ambulance. The ambulance driver was still waiting outside. The instant he saw his team come out of the house with the unconscious man strapped to the stretcher bed, he jumped back into the ambulance. The engine was still idling ... rearing to go. Ndakaripa was following. So was Winona.

"We will follow you in my car"

Winona informed

"That will be fine, Maam."

The lady affirmed Doors were firmly shut ... Engines were revved into gear, motor vehicles reversed and soon, the ambulance and a much smaller car could be seen racing their way along the highway.

It was now way past two in the early hours of the morning. Not a car could be seen traversing the highway except for those two. Twenty minutes later, doors were being flung wide open again as the ambulance parked by the front entrance to the hospital. Hospital staff raced towards the stretcher bed that had the man strapped on it. They wheeled him inside the hospital and straight to ICU. Meanwhile, Winona and Ndakaripa were in hot pursuit

"You cannot go beyond this point, Mums ..."

One of the hospital attendants said, reaching out to restrain both Winona and Ndakaripa from walking further

"You can proceed to The Waiting Room. It's over there, along that corridor ... to your right ..."

The Orderly said pointing Winona and Ndakaripa stopped following the hospital team and looked helplessly on as the stretcher bed that Dambudzo was strapped on, disappeared behind the magenta blue Double Leaf timber doors. They just stood there as if rooted to the spot. Two minutes passed. Time stood still. No one moved.

Then a nurse passed by. Winona and Ndakaripa were roused from their reverie. They started towards the Waiting Room. It was deserted. Winona and Ndakaripa took one of the couches. Winona looked around the Waiting Room. Spotting a vending machine in a corner nearby, she offered

"Would you like some coffee or tea ...?"

Ndakaripa glanced at the vending machine distantly and said

"Water will be fine for me."

"Ice cold or room temperature?"

Winona asked, walking over to the machine

"Ice cold, please ..."

Ndakaripa replied. Winona produced some coins from her purse, directed them to the coin slot, pressed a button and a bottle of ice cold water fell into the pick-up area of the machine. She reached over and fetched the bottle. She inserted more coins in the coin slot, pressed a button and a paper cup distended. Coffee was immediately dispensed into the cup. After it was filled to the brim, and the dark liquid stopped dripping into the cup, Winona reached over and fetched the cup. She walked back over to where Ndakaripa was seated.

But now she was slouched as if in prayer. Her eyes were tightly closed. Sensing a presence hovering over her, she lifted her head, opened her eyes, produced a tight smile and said

"Thanks for the water, Winona."

She opened the bottle, took a huge sip and felt instantly refreshed. She felt her tiredness ebb away. It had been a long night. Dambudzo had come home drunk and had wanted a quickie.

She had tried to remind him of what would happen should they go ahead with his suggestion, but as usual, when he was in this state, he did not listen. He had insisted, and as usual, this was the end result. She had not known who else to call, except Winona. Thank goodness she had responded to her SOS call so quickly. She had had better sense than her and had suggested they call an ambulance! She felt greatly indebted to Winona.

"My pleasure"

Winona smiled as she took a seat right next to Ndakaripa.

'Wow!! What a night!!'

Winona reflected

'What had just transpired?!!'

She wondered. Ignoring the various magazines strewn around on the tables, Winona said

"Earlier at the house, you said this was not the first time your husband had gotten like this?"

She took a surreptitious sip of her coffee. It was hot, just the way she liked it

"And I remember you mentioning something like this to me the first time we met at the restaurant."

Winona continued. Ndakaripa remained silent, watching and listening to all Winona was saying.

"You said years ago you were trying for a baby but you noticed that every time you slept with your husband, he would go into a Coma for a week."

Winona sought clarification

"Yes"

Ndakaripa said simply

"I remember you telling me that the Doctors could not explain it. And his vitals seemed normal, yet he would be in a Coma."

Winona continued

"Yes"

Ndakaripa said and took another large sip of her water.

"'It was bizarre', you said. You also said you didn't know what else to do; after all you didn't want to 'kill' your husband. So you decided to abstain. And you said you hadn't been together, since."

Winona paused as she took another surreptitious sip of her coffee. Ndakaripa waited

"So, tell me what happened tonight?"

Winona gave her client a direct look

"What set him off like that?"

Ndakaripa swallowed. Her throat was dry. She was wringing her hands in a nervous gesture And now, she could not meet Winona's eye.

"Eee ... eee ... It had been long since Dambudzo and I have met together as man and wife. Tonight, he came home drunk and suggested we do it. Initially I resisted, but upon his further insistence, I agreed."

Ndakaripa paused ... seemed to weigh her options, then proceeded saying

"Anyway, I was sick and tired of having that 'thing' come to my bed almost every night!!"

Ndakaripa's eyes suddenly became bloodshot. Winona was taken aback and blurted

"'Thing?!!' What 'thing' are you talking about?!"

Ndakaripa winced

"I didn't tell you about this before but the truth is there is a 'creature' that comes to my bed almost every night."

"Goodness!! 'Creature ...?!!'"

Winona frowned

"And this 'creature' ... what does it want? Why does it come into your bed chamber?!! What does it want?!!"

Winona looked disturbed. What had she got herself into when she had agreed to take this Case?!! For the first time Winona was starting to doubt herself. Everything sounded satanic, dark and evil in this Case!! Ndakaripa bit deep into her bottom lip. She drew blood.

"It sleeps with me ..."

Ndakaripa revealed in a low voice Winona jumped from her seat

"What?!!"

She started pacing about. What was Ndakaripa saying? She paced some more. This seemed to compose her a bit. She took a deep breath and added

"What do you mean? What are you talking about?"

Deciding to just dive in, Ndakaripa said

"This 'creature' has been coming to my bed almost every night starting three years after Tanatswa's disappearance."

She stood up and started pacing as well. Winona continued staring at Ndakaripa without uttering a word. She was too shocked for words

"It demands conjugal rights from me."

Ndakaripa continued. Now she was rubbing her back and shoulders frantically as if trying to rid herself of the feel of the 'creature' on her skin.

"'Demands conjugal rights' from you?!! But why? You are not married to it!! You are married to Dambudzo!!"

Winona remarked What she was hearing was not only disturbing, it was disgusting as it was satanic!! What was happening here? She quizzed herself

"This 'creature', what is it and what hold does it have on Dambudzo? I don't understand the link? It's substituting itself as your husband, how come?"

Winona asked, trying hard to keep her voice level and low. She could see some hospital staff passing by.

"Dambudzo says it's some family curse ... some bad spirit ..."

Ndakaripa said

"But why should you sleep with it? If it's a family curse, then what has that got to do with you? It's not your problem. It's his and his family's."

Winona reasoned. Ndakaripa hesitated

"He said since I am married to him then it made his family problem also my problem ..."

"And you bought that?!!"

Winona was outraged. Ndakaripa looked at Winona helplessly

"I love my husband, Winona, and I want to keep my marriage. When he tells me something I believe him. When the 'creature' started visiting my bed chamber all those years ago, he told me it was only temporary and if I agreed to sleep with it then that would cure his epileptic seizures."

Winona could not understand Ndakaripa's reasoning. She frowned, but decided to wisely keep silent. Ndakaripa continued

"The reason Dambudzo has those seizures every time we are together as man and wife is because it wants the conjugal rights only with me. Dambudzo was banned from ever sleeping with me, otherwise, such things would happen to him."

"Ahhhh ... !!"

Winona exclaimed This was serious. How was she going to solve this Case? She had never encountered anything like this before!! Ndakaripa kept on pacing ... Winona too, was pacing ...Then noticing a figure approach, stopped midstep. The Doctor who was attending to Dambudzo was approaching ...

Chapter 15 - The Appointment

The answer to Winona's quagmire came two days later. She had been absently sitting behind her desk, not doing anything in particular, when a thought flashed through her mind. It was so fleeting, it just went 'wooooppp ...!!' Winona literally sat up in her chair.

Why hadn't she thought of that before?!!, she castigated herself. She reached for her mobile, browsed through her Contacts, got the number she needed and dialled

"Yes ... hallo ... Can I speak to The Parish Priest please?"

Winona listened for a minute

"Yes, I'll hold ..."

Winona listened into the phone

"Father Paul speaking ...Can I help you?"

A deep husky masculine voice came on the line

"Yes, Father Paul ...It's Winona Manyame ..."

"Ah, Winona ...!! Good to hear from you!! How have you been?"

Father Paul sounded genuinely happy to hear from her

"I am well, Father!! I need your help ..."

Winona began

"Speak child, I am listening ..."

Father Paul was all ears

"Can I set up an appointment with you, Father say this Wednesday, please?"

Winona asked

"Of course, child. What time were you thinking of popping into my Office?"

Father Paul asked staring in his Diary

"2pm Wednesday ...?"

Winona suggested

"2pm Wednesday would be perfectly fine with me."

Father Paul affirmed

"Excellent!! See you Father. And thank you"

Winona smiled

"My pleasure"

Father Paul smiled. And with that, Winona disconnected the line. She was swinging in her swivel chair. Things were beginning to move in the direction she wanted It was time ... They had been in limbo for too long She knew Ndakaripa would agree to her suggestion ... but as for Dambudzo, basing on the things. Ndakaripa had said about her husband, he was sure to refuse.

Winona thought some more ...Then a thought popped into her head ...Who said Dambudzo had to know?!! Winona swivelled again in her chair

----

"So, how is he doing?"

Winona smiled gently at the lady facing her They were seated back at *Munhira Grill*; exactly the same table they occupied when they first met six months before. It was lunch time but both ladies were not hungry. As a result, they had ordered a cocktail, each.

"He is back home. He was discharged two days back. He was in a coma for a week."

Ndakaripa tried to smile but it was obvious she was still pretty shook up from the recent events with her husband.

"I am glad to hear that he is out of the coma and is recuperating back home"

Winona hesitated She took a sip of her drink

"The reason I called up this meeting this afternoon is to discuss something with you ..."

Winona looked at Ndakaripa. Ndakaripa took a sip of her drink. Her eyes never left Winona's. She was keen to hear what this amazing lady had to say. Over the last six months, she had come to admire and like her strength. She had been her rock when she thought her life was crumbling to pieces around her.

She had slowly but surely been piecing the puzzle of her life together and for that, she was grateful. This afternoon she sensed Winona had something important to discuss with her.

"I have an idea ... "

Winona paused

"An idea ...?"

Ndakaripa stared at Winona

"Clearly, basing from what you have told me and what I have seen, there is something supernatural going on in your house. Because of that, I have a suggestion ..."

Winona paused again, this time not sure how this was going to be received

"Shoot ..."

Ndakaripa encouraged

"Why not say we conduct an Exorcism like I suggested before? There is a Catholic Priest I know. He is very good"

Winona came out with it Ndakaripa was silent for a few minutes She was thinking. Over the last years she had contemplated on doing that as well but Dambudzo had discouraged her every time she suggested it. Now, Winona was coming up with the same suggestion!!

She had been thinking about it again ever since Winona suggested it at her home that time when she came over when Tanatswa was roaming the house. However, Ndakaripa remained sceptical and said

"Dambudzo would never agree to this. He is not a religious man"

"Who said he has to know? We could do it while he is at one of your businesses ... The whole exorcism process should not take more than a couple of hours."

Winona suggested. Ndakaripa was silent Again she was thinking

"You agree, don't you, Ndakaripa, that there is something seriously wrong going on in your household that needs urgent attention and the only way to get rid of it involves exorcism?"

Winona stared at Ndakaripa

"Yes, of course "

Ndakaripa blurted

Then thinking some more, her mind was made up. She said

"You know what ... enough is enough!! Let's do this!! I want to get this mess out of my life!! If a Priest can do it, so be it!! "

Ndakaripa clapped her hands in final resolution

"Excellent !!"

Winona clapped her hands in excitement. Ndakaripa produced her wicked look and said

"So, when do you propose we do it?"

Again, Ndakaripa stared at Winona. This time there was an eagerness in her voice.

"It depends on you. I have already contacted Father Paul, The Parish Priest at St Michael's Catholic Church. He said he is willing to clear his calendar whenever you are ready"

Winona informed

"That's great!!"

This time, Ndakaripa's eyes sparkled Then as a thought occurred to her, hesitated

"Ummmm ... let's wait a few days, though, for Dambudzo to get better."

Then biting her bottom lip suggested

"Why not say I call you ... say in about a week? Dambudzo should have recuperated fully by then and going back to work. I will also give my house staff a holiday ... Tanaka would be at school. That way we will not have any interference from anyone"

"Good!"

Winona let out a sigh of relief. Thank goodness Ndakaripa had agreed. She was sure the exorcism would work. Father Paul was famous in the Catholic Church for successfully performing such a rite.

"I'll wait to hear from you then!"

Winona smiled

"Let's toast"

Ndakaripa suggested, lifting her glass. Winona was game. She lifted her glass.

"To what shall we toast to?"

Ndakaripa thought for a minute, then said

"To debts being paid ... all debts ... whether financial, karma related, spiritual ..."

Winona smiled and said

"I'll drink to that …!!"

The two women toasted. They paused as they felt the liquid of their drinks tantalise their taste buds. Just then, a waiter appeared. Winona and Ndakaripa looked at him

"Can I take your Order, please?"

Suddenly they were furmished. They smiled at the waiter and unanimously said

"Certainly … !! "

"I'll have a …."

Ndakaripa volunteered first

Chapter 16 - The Exorcism

Speaking in Latin ...

"*In nomine Patris et Filii et Spiritus Sancti Amen*"
["In the Name of The Father and The Son and The Holy Spirit Amen"]

The Catholic Priest began as he administered Holy Water, then Holy Oil along the driveway and proceeded to do the same thing as he walked towards the house.

"Amen"

Winona and Ndakaripa said unanimously as they followed the Priest Father Paul was dressed in a black priestly robe that covered him from the neck, all the way down to his ankles. A white collar could be spotted anchored securely and neatly along his neckline.

He was wearing black sandals. In his hands, besides clutching two large transparent bottles - one which had Holy Water; the other with Holy Oil - he was also holding a small Prayer Book. The Holy Rosary dangled around his left wrist. Speaking in Latin ...

"*PATER noster, qui es in caelis, sanctificetur nomen tuum. Adveniat regnum tuum. Fiat voluntas tua, sicut in caelo et in terra. Panem nostrum quotidianum da nobis hodie, et dimitte nobis debita nostra sicut et nos dimittimus debitoribus nostris. Et ne nos inducas in tentationem, sed libera nos a malo. Amen*"
["Our Father, who art in heaven Hallowed be thy name Thy kingdom come Thy will be done on earth as it is in heaven Give us this day our daily bread And forgive us our trespasses As we forgive those who trespass against us And lead us not into temptation But deliver us from evil Amen]

The trio recited The Lord's Prayer as they were walking around the house with the priest in front continuing to administer Holy Water and Holy Oil on the ground as well as around the house. After going around the perimeter of the yard and the house, the trio walked inside the house. All along it had been peaceful and quiet, but the instant Father Paul opened the front door and stepped inside, all hell broke loose!!

A strong gust of wind emanated from inside the house. With shear force and energy was so strong and powerful that it threatened to blow them all away!! Father Paul continued reciting The Lord's Prayer at the same time, proceeding to enter inside the home. The instant the trio entered the Lobby, a strange eerie cry emanated from some where. It sounded tormented

"Is that the sound of a little girl? ..."

Father Paul whispered

"Yes ..."

Ndakaripa whispered back

"She sounds like she is in agony!!"

Father Paul looked around He continued administering Holy oil and Holy Water ... on the ceiling ... on the walls ... on the furniture ... on the floor ... Each time he administered the Holy Oil and Holy Water, the little girl's voice quivered as if in pain.

First stop was upstairs where the bedrooms were. When they entered the main bedroom, everything was quiet ... silent ... peaceful ...

"No disturbance here ..."

Father Paul observed as Ndakaripa closed the door and they headed for the second bedroom, then the third, then the fourth. When they came to the fifth one, the door would not open.

"Its stuck !!"

Ndakaripa said struggling to open the door

"Is this your little girl's room?"

Father Paul asked softly

"Yes!!"

Ndakaripa uttered, still struggling to wrench the door open.

"I see"

He said. He flipped through some pages and stopped at a particular prayer. He started reciting it. Instantly, the door started shaking and shaking. The sudden movement took Ndakaripa by surprise. She let go of the door and the release forced her to jerk backwards.

She could have hit the back of her head on the wall, had Winona not steadied her. The door flung wide open and a strong gust of wind blew towards them. It was so forceful and powerful it was like a whirlwind. The trio held onto each other for sheer balance. Father Paul continued to recite his prayer. After a few minutes, the gust of wind seemed to subside.

The trio force-marched their way inside the bedroom. Father Paul administered the Holy Water and Holy Oil around the room. Wardrobe doors ... books ... clothes ... were flung whichever way The trio had these flung at them by an invisible force. They had to seek cover this way and that, using their hands to protect their heads and faces.

When he came to Tanatswa's bed and performed the same ritual, a loud scream emanated. It was so high pitched and coming from such high decibels that their ears could not contain it. They had to hold their hands to their ears to containerize it. Father Paul continued reciting his prayer.

Ten minutes later, the high pitched scream and gust of wind suddenly stopped. The silence came so suddenly, was so quick and came so unexpectedly that the trio literally lost their balance. They reeled backwards. Father Paul, Winona and Ndakaripa looked at each other.

"That was a close one!!"

Father Paul tried to induce a lighter note to it But Winona and Ndakaripa were beyond chuckling. This was disturbing stuff!! When they began, they had not realised that it would be this violent. When they looked around, it was like a tornado had hit the bedroom. Sheets, pillows, duvets, books, were strewn all over. The Exorcism continued.

The fifth bedroom was followed by the lounges; dining rooms ... There was peace in these rooms. Father Paul did not linger. Last stop was the kitchen. This time, the whole house shook vigorously.

It was like an earthquake was upon them. Unruffled, unflustered, Father Paul continued reciting his prayers from his Prayer Book and administering the Holy Oil and Holy Water. As they neared the kitchen, the door flung wide open of it's own accord. It started banging against itself making a huge noise and racket. Cups, plates, pots, spoons, forks, even knives were hurled at them by an invisible force. To protect themselves, they had to duck'n'dive!!

"Its ok ... It's ok ... You are among friends here ..."

Father Paul would intercept his prayers every now and again with this statement. The ducking'n'diving continued. There was a time when the throwing of missiles was so quick and frequent that all the three could do, was keep their heads down. Some of the missiles caught Father Paul on his forehead, resulting in a nasty cut on that area. Some caught Winona at the back of her head. She had spun with shock and pain.

She had thought she would faint from the impact of it all. Some had caught Ndakaripa at her spine. She had temporarily been enveloped in a state of paralysis. She had to breathe deeply for a few minutes, eyes tightly shut, to regain her composure and locomotion. Father Paul administered Holy Oil and Holy Water inside the kitchen every chance he got. The screaming started again ... This time it was more of like a wail. A few minutes later, it turned into a whimper

"Daddy ... Daddy ... Please make him stop!! It hurts ..."

Father Paul, Winona and Ndakaripa stopped in their tracks to listen more closely.

"Did you hear that?!"

Winona whispered

"Yes"

Ndakaripa whispered back

"Is that the sound of your little girl's voice?"

Father Paul more of spoke softly, than whispered

"Yes"

Ndakaripa nodded

"From the sound of it, looks like she is stationed here ..."

Father Paul spoke looking around

"What do you mean 'stationed here ...'?!!"

Winona frowned

"I mean she is here"

Father Paul would not elucidate further. The clock struck three in the afternoon ...

Chapter 17 – Dambudzo

"Auch ... !!"

Dambudzo twitched. He was seated at his desk in his office at *Nemapare Passenger Services*. The clock had just struck three in the afternoon. He had been working since morning. He had been trying to put out fires at his company since then. Ever since the Harare - Bulawayo fiasco, business had dropped 90% as passengers literally refused to board his vans.

They had tried to attract customers by slashing their prices, but this had not worked. Still passengers refused to board his vans. Trouble at *Nemapare Passenger Services* had trickled down to his other businesses. What was he going to do? He had held his head in the palm of his hand. He was now feeling a bit tired. That itch again ...!!

'Auch ...!!'

He wriggled in his seat What was happening? Why was he feeling itchy all of a sudden? He looked at his wrist watch. He frowned He had an appointment in another ten minutes. His Chief Financial Officer was scheduled to pop into his office and discuss figures with him. He was not relishing this, but he had no choice.

That itch again ...!! What was going on?!! He scratched The itching was getting worse!! He started scratching himself ... his chest ... his back ... his stomach ...his left arm ... right arm ... his face ... head ... his lower back ... Before he knew it, his whole body and face felt like it was ablaze ... !! He was now scratching himself like crazy

"Au ... au ... au ...!!"

He kept saying Something was definitely wrong ...!! He stood up and rushed to the Gents. He opened his shirt to look at himself in the mirror ...His eyes widened in shock. He screamed ... !! Huge blotches had sprung up his skin !! He could see movement at the surface of his skin !! It was like there was something underneath !!

"Goodness, what is this?!!"

Dambudzo groaned Something was definitely wrong !! He needed to see his 'Consultant'!! He rushed out without closing the buttons to his shirt. He literally ran back into his office, grabbed his jacket, car keys, wallet and rushed through the door. His CFO was already approaching his office. When he saw what his boss was carrying, he looked askance at him.

"Not now, Edward ...!!" Dambudzo bellowed and rushed past

Edward looked confused He looked at his bunch of files that he was clutching in his hands ... then at the retreating figure of his boss. This was unlike him. Boss Nemapare hardly ever missed Meetings, most especially Meetings as important as this.

The company was hanging by a thread and he needed to do something fast if he could salvage the company from the situation it was in. He glanced towards the exit again.

The retreating figure of his boss was already rushing through the Automatic Sliding Doors. The Chief Financial Officer shrugged, turned and walked back the way he had come. He wondered what had just happened ...

"I am itching all over ...!!"

Dambudzo burst into the *n'anga*'s hut. All attempts at formalities had been forgotten Instead of his usual *'Tisvikewo, Mhukahuru ...'* , at the same time, clapping in that Shona traditional way, Dambudzo just barged in and slumped to the floor.

His skin felt like it was on fire. The itching had turned into a burning sensation. He needed something fast for his skin eruptions. He was sure his *n'anga* would give him a remedy.

"To what do I owe the pleasure ...?"

The *n'anga* looked lazily at him. He felt slightly annoyed. He did not like it when people visited his hut unannounced and without prior appointment. Made his business sound cheap and predictable.

"I am itching all over ...!!"

Dambudzo said, scratching himself mercilessly

"I need you to treat it ...!! Give me some herbs ...!!"

The *n'anga* frowned. Something is not right, he thought, frowning even deeper when he saw the large pulsating blotches on Dambudzo's skin. From the way he was scratching himself all over, it looked like the blotches were all over his skin!

"Let me consult my *hakata* ..."

He said He drew his tobacco from the pouch he kept at his side waist. He unwrapped the pouch, used his thumb and forefinger to pinch a bit of the tobacco, then directed it to his right nostril, then his left. He sneezed

"Hotsiii ...!!"

Dambudzo just looked at him. The *n'anga* rewrapped his pouch and replaced it to its usual position by his waistband. He then reached for his *hakata*, placed them in the palm of his hands, blew into them, rolled them around in the palm of his hands and threw them on the ground in front of him.

The *hakata* made a loud sound as they scattered to the ground. The *n'anga* stared at them keenly. As he stared at them, his face changed. It became contorted. His eyes became fearful and bloodshot.

"There is big trouble at your home."

He announced. His voice sounded panicky all of a sudden

"You better rush there and put a stop to whatever your wife and that Priest are up to ...!!"

Dambudzo looked confused

"My wife ... priest ... at home ...?!!"

"Yes. Whatever activity they are carrying out is what is causing you to break out into those blotches."

The *n'anga* explained. He was beginning to itch as well, but he controlled himself. He did not want Dambudzo to see him scratching himself as well. That was bad for business. He needed to present a facade of calm and professionalism all the time.

Dambudzo was silent for a minute, thinking. Surely if Ndakaripa had brought a priest home and he was itching like this, then it must mean one thing and one thing only ...

His heart beat a tard faster

"Can you come with me ...?"

Dambudzo appealed to his 'Consultant'. In answer the *n'anga* frowned

"I may need your assistance ..."

Dambudzo trailed

"I'd rather not!!"

The *n'anga* snapped Dambudzo looked taken aback. Why was the *n'anga* reluctant to come with him? Dambudzo stared at his *n'anga*. He was surprised to notice that he looked terrified!! What was going on here?!!, he wondered

"You better hurry!!"

The *n'anga* urged. He sounded impatient

"Aren't you going to prescribe some ointment for me?"

Dambudzo asked, getting ready to leave the hut.

The *n'anga* reached in his clay pot behind him, opened the lid and searched. He found what he was looking for, rubbed it to clean it of dust and said

"Here. Take this. *Itsangamidzi*. [A special dry root] *Tsenga* [chew] before you get into your car now. By the time you get home, the itching should have stopped. "

Dambudzo reached for the *tsangamidzi*. He clutched it like his life depended on it.

"Now, go!!"

The *n'anga* urged Dambudzo needed no further encouragement He sprung to his feet and literally 'fled' from the hut. What was Ndakaripa 'playing' with? He wondered What was she doing behind his back this time?!! He had to rush home to find out ...!!!

Chapter 18 - The Clock strikes Three

"Kwang ...!! Kwang ...!! Kwang ...!!"

The clock struck three in the afternoon. Father Paul, Ndakaripa and Winona listened to it for a minute. Even the energy and forces in the house seemed to be listening as well. Everything seemed to come to a standstill. No voices, no sudden gusts of wind, no disturbance of any kind except the gong of the clock striking three.

The second hand continued to move ... a second after three ... two seconds ... three seconds ... sixty seconds ... a minute after three... Father Paul seemed to rouse himself from this temporary self hypnosis. So did Winona and Ndakaripa. He glanced in his small Prayer Book. He began reciting another prayer. It was in Latin.

The house seemed to shift. The screams began again. This time the voice was no longer that of a little girl, but deeper, angrier, eerie ... that of a grown man. Father Paul reached inside one of his pockets and produced a small white cloth which he wrapped around Ndakaripa's left wrist. He sprinkled Holy Water, then Holy Oil on it. The eerie voice became louder. The whole house shook. Unflustered Father Paul continued praying.

"He is coming ..."

He said, more to himself than to anyone in particular

"Who?!"

Winona asked wondering who the priest was referring to

"The one responsible for all these occurrences ..."

Father Paul said forcing his way further inside the kitchen The strong gust of wind had begun again. Ndakaripa clutched at the white cloth Father Paul had tied around her wrist. The strong gust of wind was threatening to untie it. She followed Father Paul; so did Winona.

"Leave us alone ...!!"

An evil voice roared

"Who are you?!!"

Father Paul said, his voice even. Then sprinkling Holy Water around the kitchen, continued

"Leave this house at once!! Do you hear me?!!"

Then something unthinkable happened ... Something or someone struck Father Paul right in the face!! Winona and Ndakaripa exclaimed. They were utterly shocked!! They looked around to see who had done such a terrible thing. To their utter dismay and confusion, they could not see who or what it was.

Father Paul winced in pain as he clutched his left cheek. His nose was bleeding. He faltered a bit as he shifted his focus from what he had been doing to pay attention to his pain. His ear was ringing. He flexed his jaw. He suspected one of his teeth had gone loose.

"Are you alright?!!"

Winona asked with concern in her voice. Noticing blood trickling from one of Father Paul's nostrils, Winona rushed to him. Father Paul nodded, too dazed to speak. She examined his nose. Turning around she glanced towards the kitchen sink. Noticing what she was looking for, she rushed towards it and grabbed the kitchen tissue roll and brought it to Father.

"Here. Use this to stop the bleeding"

"Thanks"

Father Paul said as he unrolled a bit of the tissue and used it to tidy himself. He sprinkled a bit of Holy Water on another tissue and used it to wipe his nose and face. There was a bin nearby. He dropped his used tissue inside, walked towards the sink and washed his hands.He dried his hands with another dry tissue and threw the used one in the bin.

"Its becoming violent ..."

Father Paul remarked as he walked back to the counter to grab. The small Prayer Book, Holy Oil and Holy Water. The gust of wind was still raging on, but the voice had stopped.

Thankfully, his nose had stopped bleeding. That is when they heard a lock move, then the door open ... the kitchen Stable Door. Single Leaf. They all stared at it. A second later, a man was standing there. For a minute, Winona could not recognize who it was. Then as Ndakaripa exclaimed

"Dambudzo ...!! What are you doing here?!!"

Winona realized that the man of the house had arrived ... the one who was most likely to be responsible for all this mayhem. Dambudzo looked like he had been hit by a truck. For starters he was sweating profusely and breathing heavily. His eyes were blood shot ... and what was that protruding from his face, neck and hands?!!

'Yuck!!', Winona grimaced

Ndakaripa looked equally disgusted. Only Father Paul remained straight faced. The instant Dambudzo stood by the doorway, the voice of that same little girl started again

"Daddy ... save me ...!!"

Dambudzo shouted

"Be quiet ...!!"

Father Paul looked at him and said

"Is that any way to talk to your child?"

"She is not my child ...!!"

Dambudzo bellowed

"Then whose is it?!"

Father Paul asked. Before Dambudzo could reply, the voice of the little girl said

"Daddy ... It's me ... Tanatswa ...!! You put me here, remember?!!"

Ndakaripa broke down and started sobbing

"Dambudzo, what did you do with my little girl?!!"

Dambudzo swerved towards his wife and snarled

"I don't know what you are talking about ...!!"

But the voice continued

"Daddy ... it's me ... Tanatswa ... Help me ...!!"

The little girl was now sobbing uncontrollably. Dambudzo was breathing hard ... fuming ... Everything had turned helter-skelter!! What was Ndakaripa thinking, bringing a priest to the house?!! Hadn't he warned her many times before against doing such a thing?!!

'The problem with Ndakaripa is that she does not listen!', Dambudzo fumed

And who was that tall woman tugging along? He wondered. She looked familiar ... Where had he seen her before? He thought for a few seconds. Oh, yes, the P.I lady ... the one Ndakaripa had hired behind his back!!

Too many things were being done behind his back!! Ndakaripa!! There was an aura about this P.I woman he did not feel comfortable with. She was too pure ...He shivered

Meanwhile, Winona was observing Dambudzo. This was the first time she was seeing him conscious after that fiasco at this very house when he had been experiencing those seizures. At first glance he looked like a man with Class, polish, refinement.

But upon further inspection, Winona sensed a deeper, darker aura that lurked at the back of his eyes. He presented a facade of sophistication and self confidence, yet deep down here stood a man with extreme low self-esteem and a dark nature. Winona wondered what Ndakaripa had seen in such an animal in the first place.

The two were so different!! Whereas Ndakaripa was straight forward, pure hearted and kind; her husband looked brusque, rash and impatient. She met his eyes. Something inside her turned in disgust.

Father Paul was speaking ...

"Don't worry, Tanatswa ... you can rest now. Your father is really sorry about what happened more than ten years ago. You rest now ..."

Father Paul spoke softly and sprinkled Holy Water towards the direction the voice was coming from.

"I think the voice is coming from the deep freeze ..."

Winona whispered Father Paul nodded and walked closer to the deep freeze He sprinkled more Holy Water

"Rest child. Rest ..."

He said, continuing to sprinkle Holy Water He was now reciting another prayer ... in Latin ... Five minutes passed with the little girl still sobbing ...

"I want my mommy ...!!"

The voice finally said Ndakaripa stood up and faced the deep freeze. She was still clutching the white cloth around her wrist. She sniffed, planted a brave smile on her face and said in a soft, motherly voice

"I am here my little girl ... I am here. Be brave now ... It's time for you to take a deep sleep now ... Mommy will always love you ..."

"Promise ...?"

The little girl asked

"Promise."

Ndakaripa promised. A deep sigh emanated from the deep freeze; then silence. A minute later, a rattling sound followed ... then a scamper of footsteps ... like something miniature was running away ... Everyone, including Dambudzo, spun around to watch. When Winona glanced backwards, she saw miniature footprints on the kitchen floor ... making their way out ... It looked like whatever the creature was, it had bolted through The Stable Door and out into the back garden!!

"What was that?!!"

Winona asked, dazed

"The creature housed in this place used by Mr. Nemapare here to create wealth"

Father Paul explained. Ndakaripa was still sobbing. Then another strange thing happened ...Dambudzo started to cough uncontrollably. Father Paul administered Holy Water on him. Dambudzo began to shiver and the ugly blotches on his face and hands became even more pronounced.

"It hurts ...!! I feel like I am burning!!"

He cried out

"The cleansing and healing process is not over, yet ... not by a long shot, Dambudzo ... !! *Dura* ... !!" [Confess ...!!]

Father Paul ordered. Dambudzo's shivering was getting worse

"Confess, if you want your life to be spared ...!!"

Father Paul insisted Dambudzo was now breathing so heavily they thought he was going to collapse.

"Dambudzo ... do you have something to tell me ...?!! What happened to my daughter?!! What did you do?!!"

Ndakaripa demanded. But Dambudzo just glared at her.

"Dambudzo, I swear by my daughter, if you don't speak up right now, I am calling Child Protection Services and The Police!! You will rot in jail !!"

Ndakaripa threatened. That seemed to rouse Dambudzo out of his reverie. He blinked, took a deep breath, looked first at Ndakaripa, then Father Paul, then finally at Winona. He then swivelled and walked directly to the deep freezer. He opened it, reached deep down and produced a strange looking package. It was frozen, wrapped in a black cloth.

He closed the freezer and placed the package on top. He walked a few feet away from where he had placed the package and turned his back towards it as if it hurt too much to look at it. His shoulders slumped Suddenly he had aged twenty years. The trio were staring at a beaten man

"I was tired ...!!"

He began His voice was low ... so low, it was like he was speaking more to himself than to the people in the room Everyone remained silent. They were listening intently

"... tired of living from hand to mouth ... All the scrounging around ... the bickering about money ... the struggle ... I wanted out ... out of the poverty ... out of the misery ...”

He paused. No one moved

“One day, more than ten years ago, I happened to have this conversation with one of my uncles, Uncle Tapfumanei. You know him, Ndakaripa ..."

He paused, then for the benefit of the two guests, explained further

"He is a very wealthy man and I asked him what his secret was. At first, he refused to share his secret, dilly dallying this way and that ... talking about the importance of hard work and all that mumbo-jumbo."

Dambudzo produced a thin smile

"But I refused to accept his explanation and pressed him to tell me the truth about the source of his riches. I pestered him for days, until eventually he came clean."

Dambudzo paused. No one moved. No one spoke. Dambudzo took a deep breath and continued

"He told me that there was this *n'anga* who had 'set' everything up for him. He said if I was interested, he could arrange for a meeting. I said I was game. But he warned me that the sacrifice could be heavier and more painful than I anticipated. I assured him that I was ready to do anything.

Uncle Tapfumanei made the arrangements. A few months later, I met up with the *n'anga*. For my services, he demanded I bring a female black goat - a kid, not more than six months old ... a *jongwe* [cock] ... again black in colour ... a *sheche* [a hen], white in colour ...

He clearly pointed out to me that the moment I brought these to him, he would consider it as our Contract having been agreed. There would be no turning back from there, he said. The *n'anga* urged me to think carefully before I brought these items; for there will be no turning back after that."

Dambudzo firmed his lips in a gesture of determination

"But I did not have to think twice ... I had thought long and hard about this and my mind was made up. So I calmly informed him that I'd have the payment by the following day."

Again Dambudzo paused. Winona did not dare move. Father Paul was looking at him. Ndakaripa had stopped sobbing. She, too, was looking at her husband. A strange look was on her face. She looked like she was seeing her husband for the first time. She could hardly believe what she was hearing. It was like a stranger was addressing her. She had never known this side of her husband. And all this had happened under her nose!!

'Unbelievable!!', she thought

Winona was looking at Ndakaripa. Her heart went out to her. She looked so vulnerable, so hurt, so unsure of herself. Dambudzo cleared his throat and continued

"True to my word, I brought the payment the next day. The *n'anga* was happy. He told me to come back in four days' time. He said my sacrificial lamb would be ready. But before I left, he gave me a 'stick' to hide somewhere in the house. He gave me strict instructions that no one should see it, not even my wife."

Ndakaripa began to weep Winona tried to comfort her. She was shaking with shock

"Turns out the stick magically turned into the man who fetched my little girl that fateful afternoon!!"

Dambudzo's body shook. Ndakaripa began to scream

"Dambudzo how could you?!! You told me that you had no idea who had abducted our child, yet all along it was YOU and your satanic conspirators!! How could you?!!"

She ran towards Dambudzo and began to pound her fists on his back, head, face. She was punching, pounding, scratching, shrieking

"And you let an innocent woman go to jail for a crime she did not commit!! Thanks to you The St Gabriel Nursery School Head, Mrs Emilda Shoorai, spent five years in prison for negligence. A chunk of her life has been taken away from her, never to be regained again!!"

Dambudzo just remained still. He took the punches. In fact, it looked like he welcomed them. The pounding and punching continued for a full five minutes.

Neither Winona nor Father Paul had the strength to subdue Ndakaripa. They instinctively knew that she needed to get the rage out of her system ... her frustration ... her anger ... her sense of betrayal ...

Winona felt sad ... sad to see Ndakaripa suffer this much. She was just a woman who had trusted her husband all these years, only to realise he couldn't be trusted. In fact, only to realise that he was a monster, a butcher of their own flesh and blood ... a butcher of innocent lives !!

What a trying thing to have to experience. Normally, we expect an intruder, a murderer to come from outside our home; not to emanate from it!! That was a contradiction in terms.

Father Paul remained still. He was not talking; just watching and listening. When Ndakaripa eventually slumped to the floor with utter exhaustion, Dambudzo continued

"'Your sacrifice is already here ...'"

He produced a bitter laugh

"That's what the *n'anga* said to me the instant I got into his hut. A sack tied on one side lay on the floor beside the *n'anga*. As I sat cross legged to face the *n'anga*, the contents of the sack moved. Someone was wriggling inside. I could hear a muffled voice. Another man I had not seen before was standing in the shadows. He stood with a stooper. He was a hunchback. When the sack started moving, the hunchback automatically reached for it and said 'Quiet!! Or do you want a repeat of what I did to you an hour ago?!!' To which the wriggling stopped"

Dambudzo shivered in recollection

"'Had that been the muffled sound of a little girl's voice?', I asked myself. When the hunchback emerged briefly into the light, I noticed that he was short, dark, bold He was wearing a pair of navy green slacks and white sneakers ... I had looked at the sack again. It had stopped moving. 'My sacrifice, *Mhukahuru*?' I had asked 'May I know what it is?'"

Dambudzo spoke as if he was back again in the *n'anga's* hut "

At the sound of my voice, the sack wriggled again; this time more frantically. The muffled voice became louder I could swear the sound that emanated from the sack said 'Daddy ... help ...!!'"

"And you did nothing?!!"

Ndakaripa shrieked. She was pulling her hair and stomping her feet in sheer frustration Dambudzo continued

"'Could that be ... ?!!' I shook my head. No, it couldn't be ...!! Not my little ...'"

Ndakaripa screamed

"Say it ...!! 'Not my little GIRL ...!!'"

Dambudzo's bottom lip quivered

"What kind of monster are you?!!"

Ndakaripa shouted Dambudzo seemed numbed of all feeling. He continued

"'Just keep your head, Mister!!' The *n'anga* warned me 'Everything is coming out as planned. All you need to do now is wait a few minutes whilst Ripai here gets to work. You will have your sacrifice in a package shortly '"

At this point, Ndakaripa was sobbing uncontrollably. Winona walked over to where she was sprawled on the floor and lifted her. She helped her sit on one of the breakfast nook chairs. Dambudzo continued

"'Package ...?!!' I frowned, looking first at the sack, then the hunchback and lastly, the *n'anga*. The hunchback looked at the *n'anga*, who nodded in silent affirmation. The hunchback walked over to the sack and lifted it with ease. He placed the weight on his left shoulder and started to walk out of the hut. Whoever or whatever was in the sack, started wriggling again."

By this time, Ndakaripa was sobbing and hiccupping at the same time, Winona was afraid she would faint. She quickly walked over to the fridge, brought out a flask full of cold water, fetched a glass from one of the cabinets; poured water into it and handed it over to Ndakaripa. She took a sip and coughed.

Dambudzo continued. He needed to get the truth out as fast as possible. He had kept this secret for so long, it actually felt good to reveal it, finally. He felt relieved somehow, like a burden was being lifted from his shoulders

"The hunchback held it fast so that it would not drop to the ground. He was out of the hut for twenty minutes flat. This time when he re-entered the hut, he had with him a much smaller package ... the size of a shoe box. He handed the 'package' over to the *n'anga*; who took it and placed it on the floor between us. The *n'anga* then proceeded to throw his *hakata,* sniff his tobacco; sneezed and said 'Its all done now ...!!'"

Ndakaripa screamed. Dambudzo continued He couldn't stop now

"And he sprinkled some of his tobacco on the package that was now covered with a black cotton cloth and tied around at the edges. 'Hotsiii .. !!' He sneezed again This time I was too distraught and disturbed by what had just transpired to remember to clap in the Shona traditional way. I just stared at 'the package'.

How was I going to live with myself after this? I thought 'Here. Take it. Keep it in the deep freeze, away from the prying eyes of your wife and house help. Is that clear?' The *n'anga* favoured me with a fixed stare. His eyes were blood shot; his hands rough ... like he tilled the land a lot. 'Crystal ...!!' I said accepting the package My hands trembled The package felt oddly heavy. I walked out of the hut ..."

Ndakaripa fainted. Winona held her

Chapter 19 - Chimedza

"What are you doing here, Chimedzanemburungwe?!!"

Nhamodzenyika Togarasei demanded

"I did not summon you!!"

His eyes were bloodshot. And he was itching badly!! Ever since Dambudzo left his hut, he had been itching and itching and itching!! Every ointment he had applied on his skin had not worked!! If he didn't know better, it made it look and feel worse!! Now the ugly blotches on his face, hands and whole torso had turned red!!

And they were vibrating like there was something inside them that needed to spew out!! He had now stopped scratching for every time he did, one of the blotches erupted and this repulsive thick dark yellow puss would come out.

"Argghh ...!!"

He uttered in disgust and utter revulsion whenever this happened, wiping away the repulsive fluid with a black cloth.

"Sir ... Sir ..."

The miniature creature was out of breath. It looked like it had been running a mile

"All is not well at The Nemapare Residence!! I had to run for my life!!"

The creature breathed again, this time clutching its right knee in order to catch its breath. The creature had large ears ... shaped like a bat's. Its eyes were oblong in shape and looked like a cat's. It stood at an astonishing one and a half foot at full height. It had a head the size of a basketball It was as hairy as a warthog.

Upon closer inspection, the creature was inflicted with ticks all over its body. It was scratching all over. Its arms looked elongated like it spent most of its time walking on them. It had feet that looked like a human's, only hairy. The feet looked abnormally larger than the whole frame It was a wonder that the creature could stand and walk on two feet!! One would have expected it to crawl on all fours.

"What is happening over there?!!"

Nhamodzenyika asked curiously in spite of himself

"Some religious man came to the house, apparently under the invitation of your client's wife. He was throwing all sorts of strange oils and water around the yard and inside the house that made me feel very uncomfortable. Initially, I tried to scare them by invoking this strong gust of wind that threatened to blow them to kingdom come.

When they would not barge, I addressed them in this strange, evil - like voice. When that too, did not work, I resorted to slapping the religious man. This seemed to deter him a bit as he felt the pain of the punch. Made his nose bleed too ...!!"

The creature spoke in a boastful manner

"And then what happened?"

Nhamodzenyika asked. He looked totally unmoved

"There was another woman there ... very tall ... She came to his assistance by providing a tissue that he used to wipe his nose with. Her aura was too pure for me to interfere."

The creature shivered in recollection There had been something about that tall woman that made it nervous.

"The religious man recovered and continued mumbling some mumbo-jumbo prayer and splashing that strange oil and water around!! The little girl was in agony and started screaming. I could not shut her up!! The more I tried to restrain her, the more she wriggled and screamed. At one time she bit my hand, you know!! I swear she drew blood!!"

The creature felt sorry for itself as it stared at it's right index finger Nhamodzenyika couldn't care less. He was too upset with this creature. Protocol demanded that it should never have come back to him in the first place! By doing this, the creature had automatically rendered The Contract he had with Dambudzo Nemapare, null and void. All hell was about to break loose ...

He heard it before he saw it!! This sudden gust of wind ... followed by the rattling of his hut. The makeshift tin roof threatened to come undone any minute. The rafters made a loud noise as they rattled against the beams. The creature squealed, scuttled and hid behind the clay pot.

It was whimpering and trembling with fright. The 'sticks' in the clay pot started to vibrate. An enormous sound emanated from it. They were sounds of people moaning The creature scuttled away from the clay pot, whimpering, and hid behind a *rusero* [reed basket] hung on the back wall.

The hut shook. Nhamodzenyika looked up. Pebbles, rust and flakes of paint were 'raining' from the ceiling and gathering into dust on the floor. Then the

154

clay pot lid shot up and landed on the floor. Out emerged all sorts of strange looking creatures ... most of which looked like the creature that had escaped from The Nemapare household. Black smoke also escaped from the pot and started navigating about. Nhamodzenyika panicked and tried to grab the lid to the clay pot. But every time he tried, the lid would move, evading him. By this time, Nhamodzenyika was on his feet. A few minutes later, he felt a slap right on his cheek.

The impact saw his *ngundu* [traditional head gear] fly across the room to land on the floor towards the door. Pain seethed through his system. He clutched at his left cheek. No sooner had he clutched his left cheek, did he feel another slap on his right cheek. He swayed around ... shoulders bent in a gesture of ready for battle. He was looking this way and that ... He was trying to identify which of the creatures had struck him. How dare it ...!!, he fumed

'Wait till I get my hands on it ...!!'

Nhamodzenyika fumed The slap came again ... then again ... and again ...The third slap saw one of his front tooth fly to the wall and land on the ground. Blood oozed out. Nhamodzenyika screamed. By the fifth slap, Nhamodzenyika was now dazed. His whole face ached. He had bitten his bottom lip. It was bleeding profusely.

"Boss ...!! Make it stop!!"

The creature hiding behind the rusero shouted above the din.

"Shut up!!"

Nhamodzenyika snapped. The hunchback emerged He looked around the hut. He saw the mayhem and chaos. As he looked around, he saw Nhamodzenyika just standing there, blood everywhere, the left hand clutching his left cheek, whilst the right hand tried to catch the creatures and throw them back in the clay pot.

He became furious. As if in slow motion, he marched towards Nhamodzenyika ... arms outstretched. Nhamodzenyika had his back turned against the hunchback. He did not see it coming until it was too late. He tried to duck, but the man caught him just in time.

"Gotcha ... !! Finally ... !!"

He grunted. Nhamodzenyika tried to wriggle out of the man's grasp, to no avail. The hunchback was extremely strong. His grip was like vice grip. He lifted Nhamodzenyika with one arm and threw him roughly to one of the walls. The hut shook even more from the impact. Nhamodzenyika felt his head spin.

The side of the body that made contact with the wall burst into a thick yellow liquid. Puss splattered all over the floor. Nhamodzenyika screamed. But the hunchback was not yet done. It rushed where Nhamodzenyika lay in a heap, sprawled on the floor; picked him up with one hand and smashed him right at the wall, again!!

The wind was knocked out of him. Nhamodzenyika felt like a doll. This time he saw stars. He tried to get up and run for his life, but the creatures blocked the door. He was caged in!! Panic enveloped him. By this time, he was sure he had suffered a broken collarbone.

Excruciating pain was emanating from his left shoulder. His left hand lay limp at his side. He tried to bark orders, to make them get out of his way. But they were not listening. A rattlesnake that had fallen from the roof when the hut started shaking slithered its way towards Nhamodzenyika. He tried to commandeer it to stop, but it would not listen. It would not obey.

The rattlesnake lifted its head, stood at full height on its tail facing Nhamodzenyika. Nhamodzenyika looked petrified. He was immobilised by terror. One moment the rattlesnake was hissing, the next it was striking!! Nhamodzenyika felt lethal poison being injected into his veins.

The rattlesnake had bit him right on his neck!! Nhamodzenyika swayed, clutched his neck and screamed. Pain like he had never felt before in his fifty years ravaged his whole system as the poison took effect. Nhamodzenyika collapsed to the ground. He was wriggling with pain.

The noise made by the creatures was defeaning. It was like they were celebrating his downfall. The black smoke glided over the room, turned and glided towards Nhamodzenyika. It hovered over him like a drone, then plunged into him.

Nhamodzenyika caught fire. He screamed and started to run around the perimeter of the hut. The feathers he wore around his neck and torso did not make things any easier for him. They caught fire and before he knew it, he had become a burning inferno.

The paraffin lamp inside the hut made things worse. The creatures had knocked it over in their excitement. The fire spread to the face masks, to the trinkets like bows, arrows, tsero, clay pots, human skulls, bones, feathers. Passers-by who heard the scream, the shouts and commotion inside the hut ran towards it.

'Someone is in trouble in there ...!!'

One man shouted. Another good Samaritan tried to open the door and rescue the man inside, but strangely, the door in question would not open!!

'Come help me ...!! I think the door is stuck ...!!'

The good Samaritan shouted towards some passers-by. Those who were driving past quickly parked their cars along the shoulder of the road and ran back towards the hut. It had to take five strong men to finally pry and force the door open.

By this time, a man was twitching, lying on the ground. He had been badly burnt. Smoke could be seen still emanating from his body. What had been a torso of a man had turned into a heap of badly burnt flesh. They could hardly recognise his face. As the men rushed towards him, Nhamodzenyika breathed his last.

He twitched one last time and remained still. The men were shocked to also see mounds of ash spread on the floor around the hut. There must have been more than twenty heaps in total!!

'What happened here ...?!!', one man asked, looking around

The other men shook their heads in commiseration. More and more passers-by parked their cars by the edge of the road to take a look ...

'What had just happened here ...?!!', they all wondered

Someone had called The Police and Ambulance. Their sirens could be heard in the distance ...

Chapter 20 - I want out!!

"She is coming to ..."

Winona continued to fan Ndakaripa with a table cloth. She was trying to revive her. Ndakaripa moaned, placed her right hand to her head and opened her eyes. She looked dazed for a minute. She blinked. Then as recollection of the recent events hit her, she began to sob again.

"Easy ... Easy ..."

Father Paul spoke softly. He was patting Ndakaripa on her back. Winona was holding her in her arms. Ndakaripa sat up straight She looked around and caught a glimpse of her husband. *Hasha neshungu* [Her fury and frustration] returned. She cried even more loudly

"I bet you are happy now, Dambudzo!! Thanks to you, I will never see my daughter again ...!!"

"I am sorry my wife ..."

Dambudzo tried

"Don't ...!!"

Ndakaripa lifted an index finger to silence her husband. But Dambudzo would not stop

"I am sorry ... I don't know what actually came over me to do such an abominable thing."

"That's because you have no conscience, no sense of right or wrong, someone who loves money more than he does his family ..."

Ndakaripa spat. Dambudzo said

"I am sorry ... I know I hurt you and you have no reason to trust me ever again. But if you can find it in your heart to forgive me, I promise to make it up to you."

Dambudzo tried to reach out to Ndakaripa but she jumped like a snake was about to bite her. Dambudzo's eyes filled to the brim with tears.

"Please ... honey ..."

Dambudzo said

"Don't honey me ...!!"

Ndakaripa flinched. Then springing to her feet and sniffing loudly, screamed

"I want a divorce ...!! Do you hear me, Dambudzo...?!! I want a divorce!! I will not live with a monster ... a beast like you ...!! And I am taking my son with me ...!!"

Dambudzo looked catatonic. He could not say anything else except hang his head to one side and sob uncontrollably. Ndakaripa was sobbing too. Her shoulders shook with emotion

"There ... There ..."

Winona tried to comfort her. But Ndakaripa pushed Winona to one side and lunged at her husband She threw punches at him. Dambudzo used his hands to protect himself. This continued for about a few minutes. Satisfied that she had had her partial catharsis, Father Paul held Ndakaripa's right hand and restrained it.

"There ... There ... Mrs. Nemapare ... Let us device a way forward ..."

Ndakaripa looked at him as if in a daze. Father Paul continued

"First of all, I will need to do my final prayer and bless each and every one of you ... Second ... both you and Mr. Nemapare will have to arrange for a funeral ..."

"Funeral for who ...?"

Ndakaripa looked confused

"Funeral for your little girl. I take it that the 'package' on top of the freezer there is your little girl's remains ... most likely her head ...?"

Father Paul directed the last question towards Dambudzo. Dambudzo nodded. Ndakaripa shrieked. Winona shivered. What kind of man was Dambudzo? She found asking herself

"So, definitely a funeral will have to be held. Family and friends will have to be informed of the demise that befell Tanatswa all those years ago."

Father Paul stopped and looked, first at Ndakaripa then at Dambudzo. Dambudzo and Ndakaripa both nodded What the priest was saying made sense. Definitely a funeral would bring closure, not only to them as parents but more importantly to their little girl as well.

"I can preside over the funeral if you want ..."

Father Paul volunteered

"That would be helpful. Thank you, Father."

Ndakaripa said Father Paul hesitated

"There is the issue of a dare ... family confession "

"Yes."

Ndakaripa spoke

"I will get in touch with my family representative who will call for this "

"Then there is the issue of Child Protection Services and The Police. I'm afraid I'll have to inform Ms Erica Machiwenyika and Inspector Rapingwa about this Case. I am bound by law to report what happened to them "

Winona cleared her throat. Father Paul and Ndakaripa nodded Dambudzo seemed miles away. A moment of silence ensued.

"Will Child Protection Services take Tanaka away from me after this?"

Ndakaripa asked nervously. Even Dambudzo looked nervous. He fidgeted. Winona said

"I don't know. We will have to hear from Ms Erica. As you know, Child Protection Services are very strict when it comes to a child's welfare. Dambudzo had his own daughter killed; that is a very serious matter.

The fact that you Ndakaripa had no knowledge of it does not exonerate you. Both of you are most likely to be deemed as unfit parents. But as I said let's wait and hear what they say "

The house became eerily silent. A few minutes passed as each one reflected on all that had transpired. Then Father Paul opened his small Prayer Book, found the page he was looking for and began to pray, in Latin. He administered Holy Oil and Holy Water at Dambudzo, followed by Ndakaripa then at Winona.

After that, he walked around the whole house administering the Holy Water and Holy Oil and chanting another prayer. This time, there was no disturbance around the house ... no movement ... no strange sounds ... no voices. Just silence, peace, harmony.

"The reason we have called this meeting today is to discuss the issue between our in - law, Dambudzo Nemapare here and our daughter, Ndakaripa, seated over there."

Ndakaripa's uncle began Dambudzo was seated on one of the sofas, whilst Ndakaripa was seated on another one, a short distance from him. About fifty people had congregated at Dambudzo and Ndakaripa's home. They were all seated in the lounge.

Relatives from Dambudzo's side of the family and Ndakaripa's side of the family had gathered under the invitation of Ndakaripa and her family. Takesure and his wife, Zorai had also come. Takesure was Dambudzo's uncle.

Like all the other guests, they were very curious to know why the dare had been called. Winona was also present.

'I want you present for moral support'

Ndakaripa had appealed. Winona had acquiesced.

"As you all know, last week we held a funeral for little Tanatswa; the mysterious circumstances surrounding her death haunted, shocked and pained all of us. Today, we are gathered here at the request of little Tanatswa's mum."

Ndakaripa's uncle was silent for a minute as he looked around. He could see that all eyes were upon him. All the guests were waiting with baited breath to hear what the reason was. He was clearly pensive. He did not like to be the bearer of bad news, but he had no choice. It was his responsibility to act on behalf of his family under such circumstances. He cleared his throat and continued

"As you all know, ten years ago little Tanatswa went missing. Her father was supposed to pick her up from Nursery, but at the time he said he had forgotten. Investigations were carried out by The Police but they could not find little Tanatswa or her body.

The Principal of the Nursery was prosecuted for negligence, sentenced and actually served time in prison. And all this while, Dambudzo was the one behind the disappearance of his little girl. He let an innocent woman be punished for a crime she did not commit!! What a travesty!!"

"Shame on him ...!!"

One of Ndakaripa's aunts shouted. Ndakaripa's other relatives followed suit

"Dambudzo is the one *akachekereresa mwana wake kuti aprospe* in business ... [who had his daughter killed for ritual purposes so that he could prosper in business ...]"

Ndakaripa's uncle paused for full effect He was appalled and disgusted by Dambudzo's behaviour. There was a hush around the room. People started mumbling among themselves.

'Ndibaba verudzii vanochekereresa mwana wavo ...?!' [What kind of father conspires with someone to have his daughter killed for ritual purposes ...?!]

An aunt mumbled

'Ko, kubereka zvakunorwadza wani ...!!' [Giving birth is already a difficult process as it is (without the added complication of having the father kill his own offspring whom the mother already laboured for whilst giving birth to the child) ...!!]

A cousin blurted and held her bossom with both her hands in an agitated and sad manner

'Saka vanababa havachatrustwe ka mudzimba umu ...?!!' [Fathers cannot be trusted in the home ...?!!]

A niece threw her hands up in the air in frustration

'What is this world coming to where fathers kill their own offspring?!!'

One of Ndakaripa's sisters blurted sadly and shook her head. An uncle from Dambudzo's side of the family lashed out

"But how do you know it was Dambudzo who committed this atrocious act? Maybe it was somebody else ...?!!"

Ndakaripa's uncle lashed back.

"The culprit in question is right here. *Muvhunzei mega kana muchida ...* [Ask him yourself if you want ...]"

All eyes glared at Dambudzo. Whilst Ndakaripa's relatives eyes were blazing with anger, frustration and hatred; Dambudzo's relatives eyes looked saddened, remorseful and pained. Dambudzo could not meet their eyes. He continued to look down.

"Dambudzo, speak, for goodness sake!! Are all these allegations true?!!"

Dambudzo's eldest uncle shouted. Dambudzo remained quiet. He could feel the eyes of everyone there present, literally boring into him.

"Speak!!"

His uncle commanded. Dambudzo remained silent. Instead, they saw tears start to trickle down his cheeks.

"There is your answer!!"

Ndakaripa's uncle shouted, pointing an accusatory, shaking finger at Dambudzo. Everyone was silent

"Not only did he have his daughter killed for ritualistic purposes, but he had his *sitokoloshi* have conjugal rights with his wife!!"

Ndakaripa's uncle continued. This time everyone shouted a 'What?!!' And a commotion erupted around the room. Everyone looked visibly shaken.

"You can't be serious ...!!"

One of Ndakaripa's cousins blurted out

"Did I hear you right ... uncle ...?!!"

"Yes, Irene, you heard me right. What do you think caused Dambudzo to have those seizures and go into a coma every now and then over the years ...?!!"

Ndakaripa's uncle spoke with disgust and outrage

"You mean ... you mean Dambudzo was not allowed to have conjugal rights with his wife, that is why he had those seizures and went into a coma ...?!!"

Irene was incredulous

"Yes ..."

The uncle nodded

"*Nhai imi ...!!*" [Oh my goodness ... !!]

Ndakaripa's sister shook her head in deep shock

"Dambudzo how could you?!!"

Dambudzo could not meet his in-law's eyes and kept staring at the floor
Silence ensued

"*Saka* [So] what is the way forward?"

Ndakaripa's Aunt eventually asked, verbalizing what was on everyone's
mind

"Ndakaripa wants a divorce"

Ndakaripa's uncle announced A hush ensued. Dambudzo's relatives' worst
fears had been confirmed!! What were they going to do? Dambudzo's uncle
was the first to respond

"I know a terrible travesty has been committed here. Dambudzo has done a
terrible deed. I agree and I do not condone what he has done. What he did
was reprehensible, no question there."

He then directed his gaze towards Ndakaripa

"Now I am appealing directly to you, Ndakaripa ...Can you find it in your
heart to forgive your husband ... Can you please reconsider ...? I am begging
you ..."

Ndakaripa lifted her head and directed her gaze directly at Dambudzo's uncle

"Uncle Dereck, I have thought long and hard about this and the answer is NO!! Absolutely NOT!! Dambudzo is like an animal that preys and eats its young. No!! What Dambudzo did is totally unforgivable. I'm afraid I cannot remain married to a man like that!! So to answer your question Uncle, the answer is No!"

Again there was a hush around the room.

"*Muroora* [Daughter-in-law], can you please reconsider? *Handiti zvinonzi* [Isn't it there is a saying] 'to err is human but to forgive is divine?'"

Dambudzo's great aunt pleaded. But Ndakaripa shook her head slowly

"No, Great Aunt Becca. My mind is made up. I cannot. I trusted Dambudzo and he betrayed me in the worst way imaginable. The answer is still No!"

"Why take the decision now whilst you are still upset, muroora?"

Great aunt Becca tried again. She loved Ndakaripa and did not want to lose her as an in-law. Over the years she had become fond of Ndakaripa. She was kind, generous, loving, hard working. She was sure there was noone else like her for her beloved nephew.

"Why not wait for a cooling off period, then make a decision from a position of power when you are no longer angry?"

She was secretly hoping that the longer Ndakaripa delayed making a decision, the more likely she would decide to stay on with Dambudzo afterall. Ndakaripa looked at Dambudzo. *Shungu* [Anger] gripped and enveloped her She started to sob

"Dambudzo you hurt me. You had our little girl killed for your satanic purposes!! I carried that baby for nine solid months in my womb ... spent seventeen hours in labour ... and this is the thanks I get?!! As if that was not bad enough, Child Protection Services have taken our son from us as a result of your diabolical act. They have deemed us unfit parents!!"

Ndakaripa swore and lashed out

"You are a harsh, cruel man, Dambudzo ... a beast!! I don't ever want to set my eyes on you again!! Ever!! Do you hear me?!!"

Ndakaripa was now shouting and weeping at the same time

"There. There. "

One of her sisters was now comforting her.

"Well, you heard from the horse's mouth. Ndakaripa has said No."

Ndakaripa's uncle reiterated

"Dambudzo *akapara mhosva paakachekereresa mwana wake. For that anotofanira kuripa.*"
[Dambudzo committed a grievous act when he arranged to have his daughter killed for ritual purposes. For that he has to pay a fine (to Ndakaripa 's family)]

Ndakaripa's Uncle continued. Clapping in a Shona traditional way, Dambudzo's uncle said

"*Tazvinzwa Shumba. Saka mati tobvisa pakadini?*"
[We have heard what you have said, Sir (addressing him with his totem – its a sign of respect in The Shona culture) So how much?]

"*Mombe nhatu dzinotsika.* [Three live cows] *Yekutanga ndeyekuripa* [The first one is to say sorry to] Ndakaripa for the pain and suffering Dambudzo caused her when he killed the daughter she carried in her womb for nine months

The second one is to say sorry to Tanatswa for killing her. The third is for Tanaka. By killing Tanatswa, Dambudzo robbed Tanaka a sister."

Ndakaripa's uncle said

"OK. *Shumba, tanzwa zvamataura. Tichaita zvamataura.*"
[We will do as you suggest]

"You will have the cows you requested a week from today."

Dambudzo 's uncle clapped in that traditional way

"Good"

Ndakaripa 's uncle nodded. Then without wasting any more time, he reached into his side pocket and produced his wallet.

"As *Gupuro* [a sign of Ndakaripa's intent to traditionally divorce Dambudzo], here is cash in US dollars"

He handed the cash to Dambudzo's great aunt Becca.

"So it's final then?"

She muttered, having no choice but to accept the cash, then passing it over to Dambudzo

"Yes it is "

Ndakaripa's uncle said

"So, I guess there is nothing else left to say then ...?"

Great Aunt Becca swallowed

"Your nephew dug his own grave, Great Aunt Becca. Now he must lie in it ..."

Ndakaripa's uncle was unsympathetic. Great Aunt Becca and everyone there-present felt sad ... very sad ... Takesure shook his head in remorse ... Zorai took her husband's hand into hers ...She knew how much Takesure loved his nephew ...

Chapter 21 - Miracles never cease

"So, you mean all this while it was Dambudzo who was behind the kidnapping and murder of his little girl?!!"

Chief Inspector Rapingwa blurted Winona nodded her head

"Eish ...!!"

Chief Inspector Rapingwa shook his head sadly

"The things people do for money!!"

"Tragic, really "

Winona said. She felt drained. The events of the last few days had taken a toll on her.

"We will have to bring him in for questioning. From the way everything is looking, it looks like the Case will have to go for trial. He will most likely be charged with involuntary manslaughter since he actually didn't commit the actual killing of his daughter ..."

Chief Inspector Rapingwa said. Winona nodded in understanding, then said

"How many years is that likely to be?"

biting her bottom lip

"Four years ..."

Chief Inspector Rapingwa hazarded Winona was silent

'Poor Tanatswa ... Daughter to a father who was willing to sacrifice her to make money ...

Poor Ndakaripa ... Wife to a man who loved money more than his family ... a man who was willing to use his own family as pawns to make money ...

Poor Tanaka ...Now under Child Protection Services custody.

He will most likely be put under adoption ...

How sad ...'

Winona thought

She had heard of such men but had never met one in the flesh before.

Chapter 22 – Present Day

"Remember that dare held ten years ago ...?"

Zorai asked

"You mean the one between Ndakaripa and Dambudzo?"

Takesure asked. The two love birds were now back at their home. They were lounging by the pool. The event of the afternoon, earlier, had triggered memories of things that had happened more than a decade ago.

"By the way, Dambudzo served three ... four years for the murder of his daughter, right ...?"

Zorai asked

"Four years ..."

Takesure clarified. Zorai nodded, then said

"And if I remember correctly, he lost everything ... his marriage ... his son ... his businesses ... his freedom ... his friends ... after that!! Zorai added

"Yes "

Takesure nodded

"It was tragic. Ndakaripa left him and their son, Tanaka, was taken by Child Protection Services and put for adoption. She refused to have anything to do with Dambudzo's ill gotten wealth after that. When he was found guilty of involuntary manslaughter and sentenced to four years in prison, his businesses simply collapsed with no-one to man them"

Zorai nodded, remembering.

"Dambudzo went into a form of hibernation after that"

Takesure added

"For years we didn't know where he was ... whether he was dead or alive .."

"Yes I remember."

Zorai sipped her drink, thought for a bit and exclaimed

"What a surprise to see them together in that restaurant this afternoon after all this time?!"

Zorai continued

"It sure was!!"

Takesure remarked. Then remembering something Zorai blurted

"I heard though that Ndakaripa has a child with another man. I hear the son is four years old, now."

"Really?!!"

Takesure was surprised

"Who told you that?"

"Oh, I have my sources!!"

Zorai was evasive

"So, did she marry this other man?"

Takesure was curious

"I understand it was just a relationship that did not end up in marriage. "

Zorai clarified

"I see."

Takesure sipped his drink, then a mischievous expression sprung to his face

"So, do you think the two are back together ...?"

Takesure's eyes twinkled with mischief Zorai 's eyes twinkled in return

"Well ... from the way the two were touchy-feely about each other this afternoon, I am willing to bet they are ...!!"

Takesure laughed and said

"Who would have guessed ...?!!"

And sipped his drink again

THE END

www.ingramcontent.com/pod-product-compliance
Lightning Source LLC
Chambersburg PA
CBHW051412050726
47595CB00010B/4034